For Laura
for re ga *Spriz* 10/6/2017

MAYU
The Life of a Finnish Woman

A Novel

Shahzad Rizvi

Second Edition

ISBN: 978-1-300-69383-3

NOTE: This is a work of fiction. Any resemblance with living people, locales, and events is coincidental.

Also by Shahzad Rizvi

Woman with a Curve

Dinner with the Dead

Murder in the Dorm

Behind the Veil

Last Flight from Earth

Arsalan: His American Journey

Khyber Pass

The Boy who Flew and Other Tales of India for Children

A Window in the Wall and Other Stories

Scattered Petals: Collected Poems

The Last Resident: The Love Story of a British Official and an

Indian Princess

Please visit his websites

www.kahany.org *and* shahzadrizvi.com

For my Becky,
as always

The Moving Finger writes; and having writ
Moves on; nor all your piety nor wit
Shall lure it back to cancel half a line
Nor all your tears wash out a word of it.

Rubaiyat, Stanza LXXI
Omar Khayyam

CHAPTER ONE

1986 Shanni

Our lovemaking was a disaster. After the first spark of interest, my desire died down and I climbed off of her, bringing our encounter to an abrupt halt. I simply could not go on. "I'm hungry," I told a stunned Mayu, who lay motionless next to me.

Without a word, she got up, put on her robe and left the room. A few minutes later, she returned with slices of melon, smoked turkey sandwiches and coffee. We ate in uncomfortable silence, our backs resting on goose-down pillows against the headboard of the Finnish bed.

When I was finished, I reached over to the nightstand and picked up my notebook.

"Shall we go on and complete your teenage years?" I asked, turning to her.

She sat pensively, sipping her coffee and staring out the window at the oranges, reds and maroons of the falling leaves, bright in the morning light. I don't know, Shanni. I need to be in the right mood," she told me, with a touch of anger in her voice. "But I'll try."

I had known Mayu for a year and a half, and when you know someone that long, you can usually tell when something is wrong—and sometimes even the cause. But now I wasn't sure.

She said, "When I was growing up, I attended an exclusive private secondary school where everyone knew that my mother was a cleaning woman. I was a scholarship student and nobody ever let me forget it. To make things worse, I fell in love with Saku, a boy whose father was the director of the bank where my mother did her cleaning. I was, as Americans say, 'from the wrong side of the tracks' and we could not be seen together in public. I suppose he loved me, as well, but not enough to defy convention.

"So I went away to spend the summer vacation with my mother's sister, Impi, and her husband, Toini. They lived in a village in northern Finland called Arrakoski. There, in the village, I played with boys of my own age. We would swim in Lake Paijanne. Those boys looked up to me and thought of me as somebody important from the city who attended a private, elitist school. I enjoyed the status that they gave me, but I don't think it made me arrogant or a snob because I remembered the words I'd heard so often from my father—Never forget where you came from.

"As I said, most of my country playmates were boys. We danced together at what they called the country club and played organized sports. On summer nights, when the air was clear and cool, we went crayfishing. First, we would catch trash fish, spear them with sticks and then poke the sticks in the mud under water. We would have dozens of sticks all over the lake that we would check on to see if they had attracted any crayfish. In the shadows, we stole kisses.

"There was one boy I particularly liked. His name was Kalle Vilen. He lived between the village butcher shop and my uncle's house. When we were returning from the village, we often sneaked into the sauna, which was in a separate building behind his house, and explored each other's bodies."

I looked up from my notebook. "Did you go all the way with him?" I asked.

She exploded, as if she'd been smoldering for a long time. Her voice rising, she said, "I already told you, I didn't have intercourse until I was 19 and that was with Eino! Now you're asking me if I went all the way with Kalle? First, you ask for blanket permission to write about me, and then you ask me to expose myself like that—like turning a peach inside out. I don't want to go on."

She was panting with anger. In her eyes, I could see my book going up in smoke. I didn't want to antagonize her. In fact, the whole point of writing the book was as a gift and a tribute to her. Another man might buy a jewel or raise a monument for the woman he cared for; I wanted to tell her story. I wanted to explore Mayu's life as deeply as possible and share it with the rest of the world. I had met her on a raw, rainy spring day, offering her my umbrella. As our friendship grew, with each passing day, I grew more enthralled by the complexity of her character, as well as more perplexed and frustrated by her. I was curious about the life that had shaped her, which inspired me to write the book.

Our cups empty now, we sat silently on the bed. Mechanically, I smoothed out the wrinkles in the sheets. In the past, Mayu had been willing to tell me about all her affairs. Why should a simple question about an escapade with a boy make her angry now? Probably, the anger had something to do with our lovemaking—or, the emptiness where our lovemaking should have been.

I knew it was not the first time a man had lost his erection in bed with her. She had been married for 13 years. She had often told me that she and her husband had had problems in bed. If the sex didn't go well, he would say that it was her fault. Later in their marriage, he would come home late at night and paint her a vivid picture of what great sex he had had with some other woman. He figured this would arouse her. Instead, it completely shut her down. Then, the sex would be worse than ever and he would blame her; it was always her fault. Finally, he'd left her for another woman.

What happened this morning may have triggered all those memories. I debated whether I should go on with our interview this morning. I decided against it. This was a matter that I needed to handle with a light touch. After all, Mayu, the person, was more important to me than Mayu, the character in my book.

"I was so tired and hungry when I got up this morning, you could hear my stomach growl!" I said.

"You saw how quickly I brought you breakfast," she replied. Her voice sounded strained, distant.

"I feel much better now," I said, ignoring the obvious message in her tone. I then added, "Mayu, I promise you, I don't have a vampire's curiosity about your past. And my purpose in writing this book is not to expose or embarrass you. I'm just expressing my love for you."

Without turning her face to me, she slowly nodded. Then she turned, reached out and lightly touched her lips to mine. "Okay, we'll go on. But for now, can you drive me into town? I'm meeting a friend for lunch in an hour."

****

A sudden noise jerked 11-year-old Mayu from her sound sleep. *What is it?* She was lying on her side, both legs bent slightly, her arm under her head. Turning over, she saw her mother sitting up, trembling.

"It's your father, Mayu. Go back to sleep," her mother whispered in a soft, shaky voice.

"Where's my dinner?" a man's voice shouted from across the room.

That's my father, all right, Mayu thought. She closed her eyes, as though that would stop what was coming. Raija, her mother, got up in slow motion, walked over to the wood stove at the foot of the bed, and ladled a soup of pike and vegetables into a bowl. There was another drunken shout. "This friend of mine wants some chow, too...don't you, Pekka?"

Raija picked up another bowl and ladled more soup, without looking up. The two men reeked of liquor, filling the tiny, one-room apartment with the rank odor. As Mayu watched from the bed in the shadows, she felt sick with anger and fear. Long ago, she had given up her dream of a storybook happy home where children felt warmed by the love of a mother and father. Tonight, like so many other nights before, she feared for her mother's life and the collapse of all that was predictable within her world.

A bowl shattered against the black iron stove at the foot of her bed, splattering her with warm soup and showering her with broken china.

"Bitch, you gave me cold soup!" shouted Aarne.

Looking at Raija contemptuously, Pekka chimed in, "That's right. The soup is cold. And if you're going to do something about it, Aarne, do something big. It's the only way to get through to that stupid cow."

Mayu saw her mother's head jerk up, and the next second, Raija picked up the soup pot and hurled it across the room.

"Shit!" screamed Aarne, as he staggered toward his wife. He picked up a carving knife from the table and began to slash the air. "First," he said, "I'm going to slice up your face, which won't be much of a loss, you ugly cow. Then, I'll cut off your fingers one by one, and then..."

Mayu sprang up and rushed over to protect her mother. Cocking his head to one side, Pekka jeered, "Bah! You're all bark and no bite, my friend. I've paid for my ticket. When's the show going to start?"

Spitting out a foul epithet, Aarne turned on Pekka. Seeing their opportunity, mother and daughter ran from the apartment. They groped their way down to the dark basement, where they eventually fell asleep huddled on the damp concrete floor.

When Mayu awoke, her body was stiff and her mother was gone. She assumed that her mother must have gone out, as she did every day, to deliver newspapers and to clean the bank. There were noises outside and a dull light filtered through the dirty window. She thought that it would be time to go to school soon. She knew that she had to stop at the apartment first. When she tiptoed upstairs, she was prepared to find the corpse of Pekka lying on the floor in a pool of blood. Instead, she found two drunken men passed out on the floor. The apartment was in shambles.

Relieved, she decided to have some breakfast. She gulped down a few blackberries, a slice of rye bread and a piece of cheese.

Then, carefully skirting around broken china and sprawled-out bodies, she left the apartment with her school satchel.

In the gym during morning prayers, though surrounded by 300 other children, she felt alone with her thoughts. She tried to forget what had happened the previous night. The school day ahead held no excitement for her. She wondered, if I don't belong at school and I don't belong at home, then where do I belong?

In the strong morning light as the children tumbled out of the gym, chattering and giggling, Mayu's preoccupation dissipated. She hated going to third grade this morning, as much as she had the first morning she had been demoted from the fourth. She had been considered so advanced for the third grade that she had been allowed to skip it. But, after a while, the principal sent her back to the third grade, claiming that what he had done was against school regulations. This not only caused her to lose face, but also sentenced her to some long, monotonous school days. Teachers were well aware that she knew the answers. Hour after hour, her raised hand was ignored. She looked forward to the 15-minute breaks between classes. Most of the time, she would go out to a corner of the courtyard, find a ball and bounce it endlessly, lost in thought. Sometimes, she found company for a vigorous game of hide-and-seek.

When she returned home that afternoon, she was surprised to find that order had been restored to the little apartment. The men had left, the fragments of china had been swept away and no trace of soup could be found anywhere. Maybe, she thought, what happened last night was only a bad dream, a nightmare? Then everything was all right within her little world. She quickly snacked on a remnant of salted reindeer meat she found in the pantry, then dashed down the street to play some more. Other children were arriving, some with their chair-like toboggans. They decided to put the sleds one behind the other and play trains. There was a thin layer of ice in the street, a bluish ice with air bubbles beneath. It would be easy to push the sleds.

Mayu chose the role of engineer, as she steered her "train" with many inventive sound effects. In the frenzy of her play, a woman's voice filtered through to Mayu, calling her name. She turned and looked. It was the landlady, Anna Macki. Mayu climbed out of the toboggan and ran toward her.

Mrs. Macki put her arm around her and said, "Mayu, your mother has been taken to the hospital. It was one of her gallstone attacks, except that it's the worst one she's ever had. They decided to operate on her. But don't worry. It's a minor operation. I know because I've had one. Before you know it, she'll be home."

So everything's not right in my world, after all. Tears rolled down Mayu's round cheeks.

Mrs. Macki bent down and embraced her. "Do you want to go back to your play?" Mayu shook her head. "Then come. You can live with me until your mother returns."

This was the first time Mayu had been inside her landlady's house. She could not believe her eyes. There were thick, rich carpets on the floor and warm, colorful paintings on the walls—and velvet sofas. *People actually live like this?*

"My dear, relax and make yourself at home. You know, I didn't always live like this. I come from a home as poor as yours." From that moment on, although 30 years separated them, Anna Macki and Mayu became close friends. Anna was surprised at how mature and sensitive Mayu was. Anna had no children of her own and being around Mayu released a sea of maternal love in her. She taught Mayu to knit, sew and bake. She saw her own young self in the girl and relished reliving some of her childhood with her.

One night, as she was showing Mayu how to use seed stitch to shape a cowl collar on the sweater she was knitting, Anna said to her, "When I was your age, I lived in the country. My family was very poor. I grew up working on farms. As a young woman, I worked as a barn-maid at the farm of a rich landowner. I suppose I was pretty and the landowner's son, Viljo, fell in love with me. I tried my best to discourage him, but he threatened to kill himself. I finally surrendered and we were married."

"Hey, barn-maid!" came a man's voice from another part of the house.

"Right on cue. That's my Viljo." Mayu knew that Mr. Macki had come home from a business trip abroad, while she was at school.

"Where the hell did you put my clothes, you barn-girl?" The voice was closer this time.

Anna got up and went to him, but not before she gave Mayu a sad, meaningful look. "He never lets me forget my humble beginnings," she said, as she walked back into the room and examined Mayu's progress on the knitting. "The irony is that we don't choose our beginnings or our parents...so why should we apologize for them?"

"I know," Mayu said. "It's not our fault." She was struggling with the stitch that Anna had taught her.

"But Mayu," said Anna, now more interested in her thought than in the knitting, "we can rise above it all."

"Tell me, Anna, what is the matter with men? Why are they so violent?"

"Because they are inferior. We give them birth, we nourish them, we love them, and then they turn on us." She shook her head.

"It hurts me the way that my father treats my mother. It upsets me the way that your husband shouts at you. And my brother is so crude every time he comes to visit. How could I possibly have faith in men?"

"I see what you mean, Mayu, but I don't want you to become bitter toward men so early in life. I want to read you a poem I wrote." Anna pulled a piece of paper from her dress pocket. Clearly, it had been folded and unfolded and folded again so many times that it was almost coming apart. It was as though her poem were her special talisman. Anna read:

"We are travelers on the journey through life's day
Whose starting-place, at dawn, we can't control.
But the road we take and where, at dusk, we end
Is our responsibility.
In sum, 'tis not our heritage nor wealth,
nor attainment of positions that matters,

But the values we adopt that make the difference
Between a well-lived life
And one that's been frittered away
Ere we face the dark night of death."

Mayu jumped up and threw her arms around Anna. "You're so wonderful!" she exclaimed. "You have such beautiful thoughts. I wish I could write like that."

"Maybe you will, one day," said Anna, smiling. "Now, shall we visit that other wonderful woman, your mother?"

"Yes," said Mayu. "Let's do that." At that moment, they heard two men's voices raised in anger outside.

One voice said, "I'm sick of drunken brawls day after day! I prefer my tenants to be peaceful people. I want you to vacate the apartment. Raija and Mayu can stay on."

The woman and the girl looked out the window. Viljo Macki and Aarne were facing off against each other.

"Oh dear," Anna gasped.

Mayu's father shouted, "Sure! I'll get out right now! And don't you worry about Raija and Mayu. They won't stay, either. They'll come crawling after me." He swept his arms with a gesture of bravado before he left.

"But I don't want to leave here," Mayu cried. "I like the apartment and I like being near you." Anna turned from the window and held her close.

Not long after, Mayu's father returned to the apartment in a truck that had the logo of a used furniture store on the driver's door. At first, Mayu thought they were moving. But as each piece of furniture was appraised and the price agreed upon, she saw that her world was being dismantled. First, the table was sold, and then the chairs, then the cupboard, and finally the bed—it was like a slow motion amputation. Mayu decided that she was not going to cry or beg her father to stop. But inside, as piece after piece of furniture was loaded onto the truck, her heart ached. She watched as the truck moved slowly down the narrow street before turning a corner and disappearing.

Raija's operation had been a success and now she was rid of the gallstones that had given her so much pain. Anna and Mayu brought her home. Mayu had not told her mother about her father's eviction. Walking slowly and supporting her mother with her body, she took her into the apartment. It was nothing but a small, empty space enclosed by four barren walls. Mayu saw the expression on her mother's face change from shock to resolve.

"We'll have to do something about this," Raija said matter-of-factly. Then she sat down cross-legged on the floor. Surprised, Mayu looked at her mother. She realized that her mother possessed a strength that she had never understood. She felt as if a great burden—perhaps that was all her father had ever been—had been lifted from their shoulders and a sense of relief began to seep into her soul. As the two sat in the middle of the room, the poignancy of their bleak situation was accentuated by the bare walls and floor around them.

Why do we need men? Mayu asked herself. Then, she answered her own question: Perhaps to hurt and desert us? Does that mean Anna is right when she says all women are masochists?

CHAPTER TWO

1968 Mayu

For weeks, I had been crossing the days off of the calendar until it was finally time to leave for the World Communist Youth Festival in Sofia, Bulgaria.

"Mayu, let me pack your things," Eino said. "We're going to be there for two weeks, so why don't you leave what you're going to need out on the bed?" Eino was being his usual self—Mr. Organized. I offered no resistance. From a number of trips we had taken together, I recalled that my suitcase had been a disaster area. So I playfully kissed him on the cheek and let him do what he did best—organize.

We left Lahti as the evening chill was setting in. Our charter train, which we shared with 800 other Finns, took us to the Finnish-Soviet border, where we were transferred to a Soviet train. The trek across the Soviet Union was an eye-opener. The train made several brief stops, sometimes in the middle of what seemed like vast stretches of flat, uninhabited land. People seemed to appear out of nowhere to greet us with bright carnations, hugs and kisses on both cheeks.

One night, it must have been around 1:00 a.m., we were awakened from deep sleep. Minutes later, still wearing our flannel pajamas, we were standing on the platform of what passed for a station being effusively greeted and serenaded by well-meaning Russians with guitars and balalaikas. It did cross my mind that the people may have been ordered to orchestrate these welcomes for us as we passed through their towns. But, when I looked into the eyes of these simple Russians and saw the tears glistening, I changed my mind. Surely no one, I thought, would show such emotion just to satisfy an official policy.

When our train reached the Romanian border, high in the glorious Carpathian Mountains, another train, carrying African and Asian youth, arrived. We were all put aboard a larger train, fumigated and given the green light to proceed for the rest of the trip to Sofia. As East met West, the air was electric with excitement—although I got into a brief sneezing fit from the fumigation. Curious eyes drank in new colors, shapes and faces. Young men and women were all walking up and down the train—at every step, seeing a new person, a new nationality and making new discoveries.

I stayed put. You see, I had never been a mercurial type. But several people came by and talked to me. One of them was a Ceylonese lawyer. With what I have found to be the usual fascination of an Asian man for a European woman, he struck up an animated conversation with me. We had a broad-ranging discussion of the general state of world communism, and discussed both his Prime Minister Bandaranaike and my President Kekkonen.

Time passed quickly during this leg of the journey, and only once did I vaguely remember that I hadn't seen Eino for some time. Soon, the conductor, dressed in his military-style uniform with piping at the neck and cuffs, was passing through the train, announcing that we were nearing Sofia, the venue of our conference.

To my surprise and delight, there was none of the somber atmosphere that I had associated with Soviet conventions. In spite of my long journey and the gray cloud of fatigue that was enveloping me, my first impression of the city was completely positive—the people looked energetic and jovial, and the whole aura of the place was festive. There were welcome signs below the U.N.-style flags flying in the warm Bulgarian breeze. Officials—mostly young people in their first real position of responsibility—scurried around, wearing insignia and name tags, getting people settled into their dormitories. It appeared that the housing had been arranged along ethnic lines. Along with a Swedish girl, I was assigned a room on the fifth floor of a high rise that housed Northern Europeans. My boyfriend, Eino, was given a room on the third floor, as it was against official policy to house men and women on the same floor. Africans, Asians and Arabs were housed in another high-rise behind ours.

I put down my things, relaxed, and put my brush and comb on the unadorned dressing table. My roommate wandered in, smiled shyly, and when she discovered that I spoke no Swedish, wandered out again. I walked over to the main building to look at the activities schedule. It crossed my mind that I should look for Eino, but I dismissed the idea.

Just as I entered the building, I ran into the Ceylonese lawyer and a very striking man who was with him. He must have been 6'3" or 6'4", wearing a saffron robe which covered him from shoulders to ankles. His head was completely shaved and his face—especially his eyes—were intense. Although he gazed at me intently, I couldn't recognize the reaction in those eyes. My lawyer-friend introduced him to me. "This is Vajirabuddhi, our monk-in-residence."

"I'm a Trotskyite," he said sharply, as if his religious vocation was subsumed under communism and he wanted to clarify where his loyalties lay.

"I'm Mayu, from Finland. Pleased to meet you."

"I would very much like to meet the members of the Youth Section of the Finnish Communist Party," the monk said.

"I'm not a communist," I responded. "I'm just at the conference to learn. But I know the Finnish contingent. I'll arrange a meeting."

He told me where he was staying and we parted, agreeing to meet in the lobby of his building around eleven o'clock the following morning. I said I would bring the Finns and that I'd be glad to serve as interpreter, if need be. The Russian language was coin of the realm here and most of my Finnish friends had not studied Russian. As I walked away, leaving the two men standing together, there was an expression of bewilderment on the face of the little lawyer.

Travel weariness notwithstanding, the organizers of the conference brooked no delay. On the very first day of our arrival, things were in full swing. I looked at the schedule and attended some lectures and discussions about *The Eventual Peace of a Troubled World through World Communism*. They seemed promising. Eino and I never crossed paths. I did not seek him out. Maybe he knew what I was thinking?

The following morning, promptly at eleven o'clock, with the Finnish contingent in tow, I was in the lobby of the Triple A Building—I called it that because it housed Arabs, Asians and Africans. We sat down on the couches of the spartan lounge, whose furniture was designed more for utility than beauty, and waited for the monk. And then we waited and waited. There was a steady stream of people passing through the room and they eyed us curiously as we sat there—blue-eyed, blond, painfully self-conscious and so very earnest. A man of medium height, with olive skin and curly black hair, sauntered into the lounge. He scanned the row of Finns until his eyes rested on mine. For a moment, we both held the gaze, then he broke into a warm smile. I nodded and, as if a nod was all that was needed to propel him toward me, he walked over and sat down at my side.

"I'm Abdullah, from Jordan," he said with a heavy accent. "And I'm Palestinian," he added, as if I could not have guessed. All the Finnish heads turned and looked toward him, as though following a ball in a tennis match. Soon, we were in deep conversation about the Arab-Israeli conflict. I began by saying that creating the state of Israel right in the middle of the Arab states was a big mistake. He must have had me pegged for one of those Scandinavian women who were always looking for an Arab cause to bleed over. Anyway, off he launched into a tirade against Israel. The Six-Day War, in which Israel had beaten the Arabs to a pulp and pushed Palestinians from the conquered territories, had just taken place and the wounds were still fresh. Abdullah's nerves were obviously raw. His hatred of Jews was venomous.

At one point, I was tempted to interrupt him and say that he had totally missed my point. I was not against the state of Israel or Jews. What I simply questioned was the wisdom of creating a homeland for Jews in an area surrounded by Arabs. Hypothetically, couldn't it have been created in the vast empty territories of countries like Brazil, Australia, or even the United States? What about Wyoming? But when I saw his eyes burning, I just played the good listener instead. After all, I thought to myself, the people of Wyoming probably wouldn't want their state taken, either.

After a while, I began to get restless. Even one of the other stoic Finns began pacing up and down between his sofa and the door. At this point, I was seriously beginning to wonder about the monk. It was long past our appointed time and I was sure something had happened. I told Abdullah that we had to leave, but he did not let me leave until he had extracted a solemn promise that I would meet him again that evening. He wanted to give me what he called "some very important Palestinian literature."

That evening, Abdullah knocked at my door right on time. He had a pile of papers under his arm. He shifted them to give me a nervous, effusive handshake. The papers fluttered all over the floor like goose-down escaping from a pillow. I told him that I was not supposed to receive men in my room, and although my roommate archly indicated that she would go for a long walk, I knew that there was a hawk-eyed concierge on the first floor. So Abdullah and I decided to take a walk to a nearby park. As we walked, I told him that all my life I had been looking for a cause worth dying for.

"Then you have just found it—the Palestinian cause!" His face wrinkled with joy and he stretched out his arms, as if to embrace me. I simply looked at him. What did I care for the Palestinian cause that I would die for it?

"If you believe in human freedom, then you have to support the Palestinian cause," he said, immediately taking his stand at the pulpit. "The world communism movement recognizes this. Isn't this borne out by the fact that this conference opened with a condemnation of Zionism, war-mongering Israel, and the imperialist United States?"

"I don't know," I said, "whether it will become the cause in my life or not, but I do feel for Palestinians who have been driven from their homes and are now living hard lives in refugee camps. The longer the wait, the angrier they become. As a student of psychology, I can't help thinking that the situation is a breeding ground for terrorism."

"Israel is doing the same thing to us that Hitler did to them," he said. "Why isn't there a big hue and cry against what the Jews are doing?"

I responded that the memories of the Jewish Holocaust were too fresh in our minds for us to censure the Jews. Humanity bears a common guilt and it is not going to fade from our psyche—certainly not in this century. As I made my statement, there was silence for several moments. Then, Abdullah spat out bitterly, "So while the world is paralyzed with guilt about what happened years ago, it doesn't want to see what's happening right in front of its nose. Do you think that after the Palestinians are all dead and 50 years have passed…that then the world will find it convenient to grieve for them? To…what was it you said…to bear a common guilt? Is it asking too much of humanity that it care for the living?"

There was nothing more to say. We kept walking in silence in a deserted part of the park. Though the path was not narrow, he walked very close to me, his free arm intentionally brushing my hip and thigh with each step. Suddenly, he stopped and faced me, dropping his brochures again. His face became lobster red. It took me a few moments to realize what was happening. Then I looked down at his pants. They were wet. He mumbled sheepishly, "I haven't been with a woman for the last four years."

From the sublime to the ridiculous, I wanted to say, ridiculous and pathetic. I was so amused that I had difficulty keeping a straight face. "We can't go back with you looking like this," I said. "Let's sit down, so your pants can dry a little."

We sat down on a park bench that had been newly painted. The white was a little sticky. Abdullah was so embarrassed that he could only stammer inaudibly. He refused to meet my eyes. When we left the park, it was the last I ever saw of him.

****

The townspeople often told us that that summer was the most beautiful one Sofia had ever seen. It didn't rain during our entire stay, and there was no skin—black, white, or yellow—that did not delight in the muted warmth of the sun's rays. The tensions felt between Euro-communists and Soviet communists in various lecture halls and discussion groups were dissipated outside under the sun and whispering trees of the numerous parks. There, nightingales sang in harmony with the murmur of fountains and the lovely fragrance of flowers was at its prime. All this gave us a deep sense of inner peace. Although 30,000 young people had descended on this city, the streets never felt overcrowded. People were one with Nature and flowed rhythmically like a languid stream. A carnival mood swept the town and romance was in the air.

After a few starts and stops, the tour bus I was on picked up steady speed. After initial introductions, people fell into a rhythm of conversation.

"Do you know the history of the Byzantine monastery we are going to see?" a genial-sounding black man sitting next to me asked. Before I could open my mouth, he added, "By the way, I'm Thomas Gibson from Ghana." I repeated the ritual of my introduction, as I had done a million times before. I told him that I was totally ignorant of Ghana's past, but looked forward to seeing the country because it sounded fascinating.

"Ghana is such an unimportant country in international geopolitics that I'll bet you don't hear much about it in Finland," he said, flashing a disarming smile.

"You're wrong," I said matter-of-factly. "Ghana is widely reported in the Finnish media. I've followed the international policies of Kwame Nkrumah very closely." Thinking that this Finnish woman was an eager student of African politics absolutely electrified him. He talked for quite a while about how they were trying to bring the country up to Western standards. It seemed that each step along the road of change was a struggle. "The West doesn't necessarily have all the answers," I said. "And its values are not necessarily a panacea for all the problems of your country."

He smiled tolerantly. I realized that he had probably heard my little speech before from well-meaning Westerners.

"What do you do in Ghana?" I asked.

"Actually," Thomas said, "I'm at Patrice Lumumba University in Moscow, studying political science."

"Then you're practically next door to us." The bus rounded a hairpin curve and Thomas, who was sitting on the aisle seat, was almost thrown to the floor. He never lost his easy composure as he glanced toward the driver and then turned his attention back to me.

"I was wondering," he said diffidently, "if you would like to go see an African dance performance with me? It's on Friday night."

"Sure, I'd like that."

His face lit up with a child-like excitement, and we spent the rest of the journey getting to know each other and cementing our newly-formed relationship. The monastery turned out to be all that we had expected. The old stone walls, thick with ivy, served as a buffer against the world—like a hand shielding a candle flame against the wind. The peace of the inner gardens and the echoing covered walkways awed me. But I was distracted. My mind was focused on thoughts that I hoped monks never had to deal with.

It was dusk when we finally returned. I entered the lobby on the way to my room. The unmistakable figure of the monk Vajirabuddhi, draped in his saffron robe that looked recently washed and ironed, blocked my way. His dome-like shaven head was oiled, glistening under the bright ceiling light. He lifted his huge arms, pressed his hands together in a prayer gesture and uttered some incomprehensible words. I assumed he was saying that he wondered where I had been. I felt like retorting, "Where on earth were *you* when we were supposed to meet?"

He had a very good explanation, but I did not believe a word. As I listened, we walked out of the building. People looked at us curiously. We were an odd couple—an Eastern monk with a Western blonde one whole foot shorter, taking a stroll in the garden. Approaching darkness and the fluorescent light from the lamp-posts heightened our contrast. We walked the length of the building until people and lamp-posts became scarce. Suddenly, the bulk of his enormous body thrust me through a doorway and we were alone in the pitch dark. I could hear his heavy breathing, as my feet left the ground. I was pinned to the wall, as he tore at my skirt, trying to get his hand between my thighs.

My first reaction was not fear but disappointment. I had hoped that this monk would be different—a nobler, more philosophical man, not a dirty, violent pervert like all the rest. And here I was in a grimy stairwell, with his sweaty body squashing and kneading me relentlessly. He was so strong that I thought I would collapse. If I scream, I thought, and am rescued, the Finnish contingent will hear about all this. They'll say, "It serves you right for cavorting with foreign men. Aren't your own people good enough for you?" And Eino... What will Eino say?

Struggling was not working. I decided to do what I did best—talking—to try to break through and make an impression on his fevered mind. I said, "This is ridiculous! Things can be arranged better than this. And you're going to have to learn to treat women differently if you want to make anything happen."

My words did get through. He let me slide down until my feet were back on the ground. I straightened my clothes.

"Yes, I guess we could try to meet another night," he said, out of breath.

I wasn't sure I liked the sound of that, but I was relieved that I had stopped his onslaught. I just wanted to get away from there as fast as possible, and I did.

The next evening I waited for my Ghanaian friend Thomas in my room. My roommate was off on some mysterious errand, with a sly smile and a pipe in her knapsack. Thomas was prompt and we took a bus downtown to see the African dance performance I had been looking forward to. When we got off at the bus stop, we dashed down the street because we were getting late. Outside the auditorium, we nearly ran into a handsome athletically-built African man. Thomas introduced him as Richard Taki from Tanzania, a fellow-student at Patrice Lumumba University.

"Would you like to join us?" Thomas asked him. I was secretly pleased that Richard consented. Thomas was too open-hearted to even think of keeping me all to himself. In the auditorium, the two men seated me between them. The performance began. The rich primary colors of the costumes, the beating drums and the languid movements of the dancers were all very interesting, but I couldn't concentrate. The whole time I was aware of Richard's presence. My arm was touching his on the armrest between us and the feeling electrified me. I was weak in the knees with desire and had no idea what was happening on stage.

"Shall we go have a drink?" Thomas's voice jolted me out of my beautiful feeling. The house lights were up, the curtains were closed and the dancers had left.

"I'm sorry it's over," I said dreamily. The two men thought I was talking about the performance.

"Yes," said Richard, "It's over and I must go." He stood up and stretched his magnificent body.

"Join us for a drink," Thomas said weakly.

"No, no, you two enjoy yourselves. I must go." Richard's voice had a tone of finality. He left unceremoniously. His departure saddened me and I felt no enthusiasm for the rest of the evening. But Thomas didn't sense what was going on in my heart. All evening he was his genial self, amusing and entertaining me. If one joke wouldn't work, he would come up with another and another until a smile would spread over my face and I would begin to laugh. He succeeded in banishing my gloom. We drank like capitalists and went back to our rooms feeling very warm and happy.

That night, when I lay down on my bed and turned off the light, sensual thoughts of Richard visited me. I wished he were there next to me. My skin tingled as I imagined his touch.

I woke up, however, thinking about the monk. I was still angry at him. I had no desire to see him again—especially since I had developed a crush on Richard—but I knew myself well enough to know that my anger would not subside until I confronted him. I was afraid that his behavior was going to taint my regard for Eastern philosophy and religion. I knew that that would be a shame because I'd always had a soft spot in my heart for the Orient.

When the monk sought me out as a prelude to our going out, I lit into him. My rage kept flowing out like lava and, in its wake, the huge figure of the monk crumbled. I shudder to think now what I sounded like, or how much of what I said he actually understood. But one thing was clear—my message had gotten through. I could see it in both his face and the embarrassed twitches of his body.

Once the storm had passed and I was calm again, I noticed with some satisfaction that he looked properly chastened. So, I agreed to go out with him after all.

The monk and I went to a café downtown and he ordered the cheapest cut of beef on the menu. He told me that—between the exchange rate and his vow of poverty—he didn't have much money.

"When I was twelve years old," he told me, "my parents tried to railroad me into an arranged marriage. I became a monk in protest and have been one ever since. Now, I'm 28. Currently, I'm studying at a university in northern India where there's no opportunity to meet women."

The waiter brought our meals and we ate without much conversation. I watched a group of six or eight people across the room, singing and laughing as they ate. Then I looked back at the monk, his head bent over his plate, so pale and lifeless in comparison. When we left the cafe, it was late and no buses were running. In the quiet, I was able to forget about my previous tumultuous encounter with the man. The change that had come over him made him seem the opposite of the bully he had been the other night. Now, he seemed smaller, more vulnerable, cuddly even. I felt sorry for him now that I had heard his life story. I felt compassion because his youth was slipping away and he had still not known a woman. He told me that he was contemplating leaving his vocation to get married.

I reached over and took his hand. I could tell that this was the first time this had ever happened to him. It was clear that he was investing this gesture with a lot of meaning. His eyes softened, as he became lost in a fantasy of building a future around me. He told me that my image, complete with fair skin, blond hair, blue eyes, and pink cheeks, looked fairy-like, as though I had come from some distant land of enchantment. When we finally parted at the door of my dorm, it was with great reluctance on his part. He slowly walked away, still spinning his vain dreams.

Back then, I thought I just didn't have the heart to puncture his bubble. Now, I realize that I enjoyed the control I had over him. What lies we commit in the name of the human heart!

****

The auditorium was buzzing with excitement. Rudi Dutschke, leader of the East German branch of the radical student movement Students for a Democratic Society (SDS), was going to speak. It was nearing the end of the conference, and Eino and I were together for the first time. Did I say why we found being together so hard? Well, there's time enough for that...

Anyway, Eino and I found seats right in the front row. As the speaker was about to be introduced, Richard Taki walked in. He sat down on the seat next to me. It was the only vacant seat in the whole auditorium. I couldn't believe my luck. This is what they mean by Fate, I told myself.

As I was introducing Richard to Eino, the lecture began. Dutschke was a forceful speaker. He launched right into an attack on the Soviet Union, the Stalinist purges and the economic failure of the Marxist system. Suddenly, two men rushed to the stage and began to pummel Dutschke with their fists. Momentarily frozen with shock, the audience came alive and pandemonium broke out.

"Let me get you out of here," Richard said to me, pulling me to my feet. I turned and looked toward Eino.

"I want to stay here and watch this spectacle to the end," Eino said coolly, keeping his eyes riveted to the stage. I wanted nothing better than some time alone with Richard. We walked out of the auditorium, stepping over upturned chairs in our way. The noise of shouted obscenities, breaking wood and flesh striking flesh followed us, as we left the brightly-lit building for the moonlit street.

"Alone at last," I said. I took a deep breath to quiet my nerves and exhaled slowly.

"My sentiments exactly," said Richard. "I didn't realize that you felt the same way."

"I don't believe in playing games. I want you to know that I felt strongly attracted to you when Thomas introduced us that night. I was sad when you left so abruptly and I gave up all hope of ever meeting you again. It was a stroke of luck that the only seat available in the auditorium was next to me…and you came there to sit down."

"That is what we call Fate, Mayu," Richard said.

"I had the same thought," I told him, smiling.

"I've thought about you constantly since we met," Richard said. "But I had no hope of ever getting to be friends with you. I thought you were Thomas's friend…" His voice trailed off. As we talked, we entered a large park. The soughing of the wind in the trees sounded like the sound of waves softly breaking.

"I had just met Thomas here at the conference," I said quickly, "and I never wanted him to be anything but a friend."

"What about Eino, then?" he asked.

"Well, that's a *long* story," I said.

"We have all night," he responded, with a chuckle.

"Then I'll talk all night," I said. "That's one of the things I do best."

"Just so long as you finally get around to letting me know what Eino means to you," he said.

"Somehow," I said, "my relationship with Eino has become bound up with my university education. I'll explain what I mean and then you can draw your own conclusions about what he means to me…and what I mean to him, for that matter.

"I graduated from high school in 1964, and found a job in a soft drink factory. That was in my hometown, Lahti. I thought that if I worked all summer, I would be able to save enough money to attend university in the fall. I knew that any university in Finland would accept me—I had been one of the top students in my class—but I certainly didn't want to go to a metropolis like Helsinki. I don't like big cities and there was also the matter of the money, so I applied to Jyvaskyla University. It's a small-town school, about 120 kilometers from Lahti. I was promptly accepted and began my studies that fall.

"I rented an attic room in a house in town and ate in a cheap cafeteria every day. I took majors in psychology and Finnish. I enjoyed the anonymity at the university. For eight years, I had

23

had the dubious distinction of being the poorest student in an exclusive secondary school, and I had hated it. All I wanted to do was study, and study I did—I got the highest marks in my class. I carried a load of 30 to 36 hours and took exams every month. These were the exams we took to fulfill the requirements for each major, which brought us closer to graduation. I was taking exams every month, while most students didn't start thinking of them before the year's end.

"So, when the boat of my life was sailing along on the placid sea of academia, I heard about a Temperance Club on campus. It intrigued me because the sole raison d'être of this club was to teach people how to have a good time without drinking. Alcoholism is a big problem in Finland—all over Scandinavia, as a matter of fact—and my own father was an alcoholic. So, in spite of my initial decision to keep a low profile at the university and not get involved in any political activities, I decided to join this club. It was too late to save my father, but, I thought…maybe I can catch someone else before he drowns? My zeal and sense of mission were soon noticed by other members of the club, and I was chosen President.

"We met often and did our share of proselytizing. But that wasn't all. We tried to demonstrate that there were alternatives to sitting around drinking. So, we organized walking marathons. The response of our members was so tremendous that our club won in the university competition. It was during those walks, which became a regular feature of Temperance Club activities, that I noticed a dark, skinny, intense man walking next to me. I was 18 at the time and he seemed a couple of years older. Soon, it was obvious that it was no accident that he was always next to me—no matter how slow or fast I walked. Whatever the club's purpose, this man had his own goal—to strike up a conversation with me.

"My social life at that time was empty and he had no difficulty walking into the vacuum. We began to see a lot of each other. Although Eino was ahead of me in school, I soon caught up with him. My life began to change. Some of this was Eino's influence and some was my own blossoming. I began to break the shell around me, make friends and free myself from my complexes—especially the 'poor girl' syndrome. Since I was a psychology major, you can imagine how enamored I was with 'complexes' and 'syndromes' and the like. I began to participate in political and social activities on campus.

"The first year had gone by and the second was underway. It was 1965. I lived in a dormitory now, and so did Eino. One Saturday night when my roommate was away for the weekend, I insisted that Eino spend the night with me. Since puberty, I had engaged in sexual exploration, but now I felt that the time had come to experience the real thing. I don't mean to say that I twisted Eino's arm—he was a willing enough partner in crime—but he did need a little coaxing. It was during our lovemaking that I realized that it was also Eino's first time.

"The following morning, my mother was visiting and I was serving coffee. She took a sip, gazed at me and said, 'My girl is not a girl anymore.'

"'What do you mean, mother?' I asked.

"'I see it in your eyes, in the way you carry yourself,' she said.

"Then, in walked Eino. He had gone over to his room to change his clothes. My mother turned to him and said in a kind but firm tone, 'Don't hurt my little girl, Eino. Keep God in your mind and your pants on.'

"That was my initiation to sex. I discovered that I had a strong sex drive. For better or worse, Eino was my boyfriend now, so he became the recipient of all my sexual urges. But I would never have anticipated his response. Instead of meeting my desire with desire, he would lecture me.

"'Sex is only for procreation,' he would say. And when I became insistent, he would brandish the Bible in front of my nose. When my frustration got so bad that I could not sleep, he accused me of being weak and not wanting to try harder.

"At my age, I said to myself, who can know all the pros and cons of sex? So I deferred to Eino. But deep down in my heart, I continued to believe that there was something seriously wrong with his beliefs.

"During this period, my libido found an opportunity for expressing itself through a debate which had arisen on campus—whether condom machines should be installed in men's rooms. I wrote an article in the student magazine saying that, if condom machines were indeed installed in rest rooms, men's or women's, it would be equating sex with—as I put it after hunting around for the right words—'pissing and shitting.' Therefore, I concluded that condom machines should be installed in gardens and lounges, surrounded by flowers and beautiful art objects, to give sex its due place in our psyche and society as the beautiful act that it is. I wrote that if people felt too shy to get condoms in public, they could always call me and I would be more than happy to do it for them.

"The reaction to the article was instantaneous and I became an overnight celebrity on campus. But, as you might have expected, poor Eino was livid.

"'How can you write such filth?' he asked me. 'And what really surprises me is that you offered yourself as a public procurer of condoms!' When my new-found fame led to invitations for public speaking and my election to the Student Parliament, he was beside himself.

"Our sexual incompatibility was heightened because he was an obsessive-compulsive personality. He would color-code picture slides before storing them, put his shoes neatly in a row with the laces tied in bows, keep different kinds of underwear in different drawers to make absolutely sure that they didn't get mixed up, order his clothes in the closet so they were all facing the same way, keep the living room immaculately clean...well, you get the picture. It drove me crazy. Every time I was in his room, I had to watch the movements of my body for fear that I would destroy the order of his microcosm. Maybe if I breathed too hard, he would sneeze!

"When I couldn't take it anymore, I suggested a break-up. Leave it to him to sing the same old refrain...'You're weak, Mayu! You don't try hard enough.'

"*Weak?* I didn't know what to think anymore. In the past, I had believed Eino and blamed myself for the problems we had in our relationship. After all, perhaps he was right and God had created sex solely for procreation. If I wasn't willing to accept that, physically or emotionally, the fault must lie with me, right? If Eino tended to be neat and orderly and I bordered on sloppy and disorganized, all I could do was question myself. But deep down, I didn't feel wrong. I didn't feel weak. I just felt different.

"We had been seeing each other for two or three years. Gradually, we had grown apart. No, I was not wrong. Still, I didn't have the courage to end our affair.

"Perhaps what Eino and I had would have continued in its insipid little way, if fate had not intervened. A youth organization that we both belonged to offered us the opportunity to travel to the United States and work as camp counselors. I welcomed the job, thinking that it would dissolve the tension between us—at least during the upcoming summer. Since Eino had initiated the trip to the States, I was not afraid he would suspect me of engineering a separation.

"You see, as it turned out, we didn't spend the summer together. Eino was assigned to New York, while I was sent to Oregon.

"We took a boat from Helsinki to Lubeck and spent two nights in East Berlin. We hitch-hiked to Warnemunde and took a boat from there to New York. While Eino stayed in Harlem, dealing with tough slum kids who opened his eyes to the rawness of life, I flew to Oregon and found myself in a very pleasant girls' camp 60 miles from Portland. We had a lake with rowboats, horses, miles of wilderness trails, bonfires, and cookouts. For the first time in my life, I made girlfriends. It seemed I was always contorting my lips to articulate the American sounds correctly, but I was enjoying myself.

"As I was having the time of my life with this pastoral existence and the separation from Eino, I received a letter from Jyvaskyla, informing me that a psychology course that I was required to take had been rescheduled. The letter indicated that if I did not immediately take the course, my graduation would be delayed a year.

"Panic set in and I wrote to Eino in New York. He wrote back by return post, saying that he would get me money for the trip home. I arrived in New York and, just as my bus pulled up to the hotel, I saw Eino come out with two girls.

"'We're going to Radio City Music Hall,' he said, adding, 'I have my plane ticket, but money for your ticket hasn't yet arrived from Finland.' He left, leaving me standing there flabbergasted.

"'We have no provision and no funds for such cases,' the Finnish Consul told me when I approached him at the Consulate. But when he saw my red face, my puffy eyes and the tears that I couldn't control, he added, 'But I can give you the money from my own pocket. How much do you need?'

"I blurted out the exact amount of the ticket, not thinking that traveling entailed other expenses. Of course, the Consul didn't know that my estimate was too low. He simply took my word for it. He buzzed an aide who disappeared down the dim corridor and returned in five minutes with the cash.

"'You see,' said the Consul, with a wry smile, 'my wife holds the purse-strings in this family.'

"I thanked the man profusely and took my leave, glad to have found one friend in my time of trouble. I got my plane ticket with Icelandic to Luxembourg, but I didn't have taxi-fare to the airport. In my pocketbook, I had a check for $25 that had been given to me as a bonus when I left the camp. I took it to the nearest bank—only to see its massive door being closed when I was no more than ten meters away. Banking hours were over for the day and even though I ran, I was too late. The door closed in my face. I pounded hysterically on it. A security guard came out and told me what I already knew. I showed him my check and told him that I was in trouble...that I *had* to have the money.

"I suppose he took pity on a damsel in distress. Anyway, he went back into the bank. Shortly, he came to the door and beckoned me to follow him. He led me into a wood-paneled room where the manager on duty was sitting at his desk, his fingertips studiously touching in an attempt to look professional.

"'Thank you for seeing me, Mr. Pease,' I said.

"He looked startled that I knew his name. Then he glanced down at the nameplate on his desk and smiled. He looked as though he had been waiting all day to do one gesture that would prove that he was a human being.

"So, Mr. Pease cashed my check and I had all of 25 dollars in my sweaty little palm. After his shenanigans around town, Eino came to my room at the Y to visit...as if nothing had happened. I was furious with him.

"I finally arrived in Finland, after hitch-hiking across half of Europe with no money at all. I was hungry, thirsty and cold, and steaming over Eino's callousness. If Eino were poor, it would have been a different story, but he wasn't. I began to see that people like Eino, who were moral without being humane, had very ugly blind spots. I began to look for a way out. But I guess inertia set in and I never ended up leaving him. Now, *cheri*, you know every sordid detail about my relationship with Eino."

"Yes, I do," Richard said, with a laugh. He reached out and took me in his arms to kiss me. I had never experienced anything like that kiss before. It sent such tremors down my spine and all over my body that I began to shake.

"Do you realize," he said, letting me come up for air, "that you have been talking non-stop for the last two hours?"

"I'm sorry," I said. "I didn't give you a chance to talk."

"Since we're going to be friends," he said, "I'll have lots of opportunities to get my two cents' worth in." He was whispering sensually, his lips lightly touching my ear.

It must have been late because only one or two people still wandered through the park. From the boulevard beyond the park, the sounds of a small brass orchestra enlivened the sleepy night. A few cafés were still open and the happy laughter of late-night customers blended with the tinkle of glasses. I had become quiet after reciting the Eino saga. We got up and began to walk again, hand-in-hand this time. Occasional passers-by eyed us with curiosity—interracial couples were still rare in those days. Now, Richard was doing most of the talking. Everything he said gave me insight into his powerful mind. Earlier, he had listened to me patiently, calmly. Now, I was listening to him with excitement and eagerness. A point came in the night when we began to talk back and forth with such ease that it was as though we were two parts of one huge mind stretching over the park, over the boulevard café with its brass band, over the beautiful city of Sofia. And then, we gradually became quiet until our messages became silent ones.

We were like two amoebas—feeling every sensation in a warm tropical sea, moving as the tides moved. The moon and stars crowned us. The breeze and dark greenery mirrored the sensuality of our bodies. In the middle of the park, oblivious of the world passing by, our bodies blended together until I saw meteors shooting through the galaxy. My skin felt such sensations that my whole body was engulfed in pleasure. It was the most beautiful night of my entire life. Perhaps that is why I cannot really describe it. In the end, words are good only for describing things you want to control or shed. Richard was too dear to me—*is* too dear to me—for me to ever put my feelings into words.

****

When the conference came to an end, I wondered what it had all been about. My monk came to see me and brought me a kilo of Ceylonese choice tea, clearly a prized possession of his. He mumbled something about marriage, while I smiled and glossed it over. Thomas also came to see me, and in a genial tone, promised to write me from Moscow. Although my heart now belonged to Richard, I couldn't find him anywhere. Even as I hoped he would appear, I began to accept his departure as inevitable. It was an almost unbearable weight. As my train was pulling out of Sofia station, I kept looking out of the window. Is that him by the newspaper kiosk? No. Or coming through the gate? Or driving into the parking lot in the Mercedes? In the three-piece suit? Mad! Mad! I grew desperate behind my calm face. I felt two things simultaneously: I felt betrayed, and I felt the wisdom of his abrupt departure. Some things were better finished cleanly—no matter how much it hurt.

Gently, I laid my head on Eino's shoulder. Poor Eino—he thought that I had drunk in too much communist ideology in two weeks and was ready for a nice long sleep on an uneventful trip home.

CHAPTER THREE

1982 Shanni

When I tell friends how I met Mayu, they are often surprised. It is not unusual to meet a woman down Aisle 13 of the grocery store next to the Tide display, but to meet a drenched woman on a sidewalk in a pouring rain and then go on to explore her life intimately is not exactly an everyday occurrence. Yet this is how it happened.

March was coming in like the proverbial lion and a gray Washington rain, mixed with sleet, was spitting out of the unfriendly sky, making the going difficult for pedestrians and motorists, alike. I had braved the weather to find some Mexican food to satisfy my ravenous appetite. Sheltered by an umbrella, I was picking my way along the street in Rosslyn on the way to the restaurant. A woman walking on the sidewalk on the other side of the street caught my eye. She was not carrying an umbrella, while rivulets of water were coursing from the strands of blonde hair that had broken loose from her ponytail and were hanging down her fair face.

I looked away from her to watch my own steps on the treacherous pavement, but her image had burned itself into my mind. Intrigued, I looked back. Suddenly, I could not take my eyes off her and a mysterious magnetic pull drew me straight to her.

"Please take this umbrella," I said without any preliminaries, thrusting the black umbrella under her nose. "You're getting all wet."

"Who are you?" she asked, with an undertone of suspicion in her voice.

"My name is Shanni," I said. "I teach the Urdu language at the International Language Institute."

"What a coincidence!" she exclaimed, finally accepting the umbrella. "I teach Finnish there." With an ambivalent smile, she held the umbrella over both our heads. Then, she added, "I'm going over to Maryland to get my car out of the shop. Give me a call. Perhaps we can have coffee or something. My name is Mayu Larsen." She walked away very quickly. I stood under the downpour, watching her ponytail, tennis shoes and drenched blue jeans that outlined the roundness of her bottom fade into the distance.

I was going to call her at her office, but I found her home number in the phone book. When I called, a young male voice answered the phone. I asked for Mayu Larsen and he shouted, "Mom! Telephone!"

There was a pause of at least half a minute, then a female voice answered, "Hello?" Mayu sounded reserved. I began to wonder if I had made a mistake by calling her.

"I'm the man with the umbrella," I said.

"You *were* the man with the umbrella," she laughed.

"You suggested that we have coffee or something sometime," I said. "Would dinner qualify as something?" I heard complete silence for a full five seconds. Then Mayu gently laughed.

"It can," she said, markedly more accessible. We set Friday at seven o'clock for our date.

When I arrived in a three-piece suit at her house in Annandale, I brought along a picture that had been taken of me with President Reagan at the White House. I took Mayu to Chez Francoise, a French restaurant near the White House where people went to see and be seen. Diane, the hostess, co-owner and guiding light, escorted us to our table, saying to Mayu, "You're with the nicest man in Washington."

People at the adjoining tables craned their necks to get a closer look at whom Diane was talking about. I felt embarrassed. Mayu looked skeptical, then her pale face went blank with the absentness of one deep in thought. She decided against ordering a drink, so we played with our tumblers filled with ice water. Looking around at the people, decor and photos of Washington politicos hanging on the walls, we carried on a strained conversation. The onus of making conversation seemed to be solely on me, but every time I opened my mouth to say something, there would be a puzzled, critical look on her face.

Like a battered fighter saved by the bell, I was relieved by the arrival of the appetizers—a salad for her and an onion soup for me. My words became few and far between, as I was preoccupied with the strands of golden-brown Gruyere on top of the soup. The main course turned out to be an even greater savior. While Mayu's task was the simple matter of easing her fork through a buttery fillet of flounder, I had mercifully recalcitrant quail bones to contend with. When we voted in favor of no dessert or coffee—a lucky consensus—we walked out; I took a breath of fresh air and sighed.

Perhaps the evening can still be saved, I kept thinking, as I drove her from downtown Washington across Key Bridge to the Virginia suburbs. If only she would take upon herself the burden of conversation or introduce a topic we could discuss harmoniously! But she did not.

As we got out of the car and she invited me in for a few minutes, I remembered my photo with Reagan. That will definitely make a great conversation-piece, I said to myself, and picked it up from the back seat. Mayu's house was a split-level rambler and a short flight of wooden stairs brought us to the living-room. On the right, I could see the kitchen with its sink full of pots and pans—a reminder that behind every working woman is a messy kitchen. I noticed she didn't apologize for it, as many women would have.

"Have a seat," she said, gesturing to a cream-colored love seat with patches where the fabric had worn away. "Would you like some cloudberry liqueur?" she asked.

"I'd like nothing better," I replied, not entirely sincerely. As she disappeared into the next room, I stood, holding the framed photo under my arm, facing the couch and contemplating the best location for the display of the photo. The side to my left seemed the most logical place since there was a floor lamp there. I walked over, turned around and dropped myself down on the couch. When my rear touched the seat, its cushions gave way and I continued to sink.

I was feeling like a man being swallowed by a giant Venus fly-trap when Mayu walked in to find me in my ludicrous position.

"The straps under that side are broken," she said, with an amused smile. "Liqueur," she reminded herself, with a whimsical finger in the air, and turned to the bar. I extricated myself, glancing around nervously to make certain that no one was witness to this embarrassing scramble. She handed me a tiny glass and sat down next to me.

"Cheers." We clinked glasses. The sweet viscous liquid traveled to my throat where it stopped in a nervous lump. I did not want to draw her attention to my bobbing Adam's apple and thrust the photo in front of her face, as if drawing a curtain between us.

"So, this is your photo with Reagan," she said in a tone untouched by awe or excitement. I felt the liqueur travel down toward my stomach, leaving a trail of warmth behind. Since she did not take the photo from my hand and looked away, I put it down on the marble top of the coffee table. She leaned back and gazed into space. Then she smiled wryly and said. "When I was married to Robert and he still worked for Nestle, we were invited to dinner at the Reagan White House. I simply refused to go. I don't like the man's philosophy or politics. Robert was very upset—the perks of success meant a lot to him—but he didn't push me. So we went to the Kennedy Center instead and saw something by the Washington Opera." Mayu talked as though I were not even in the room. She lowered her eyes, took a swift glance at the photo and said. "I really don't like the man."

So much for the photo, I said to myself. All my hopes of making it the center-piece of the conversation and impressing this difficult woman were dashed. I thought I'd be out of my mind to go on and tell her that I had been in the White House as Reagan's Urdu interpreter. The smartest thing, I decided, would be to bring the evening to an end and go home—which I did.

That night, lying in bed, I tried to analyze Mayu. The more I thought of her, the more I realized that I had never met anyone like her before. In a city where women—especially middle-aged women—outnumbered men by far, women generally sought to be pleasing. But she had chosen to be blunt and outspoken. On our first date, she had disagreed with me all evening—even to the point of belittling my work in the White House. She had certainly risked not being asked out by me again.

In the silence of the late night, my thinking finally settled down to three possibilities. Either she was very tactless, she did not think much of me, or—as I preferred to believe—she was the most honest person alive. The three possibilities turned round and round until they became a dizzy circle. I just didn't know what to think. Whatever the case, it was clear that she was intriguing, if disobliging. A woman who had left me thinking so very much about her after just one date could not be easily dismissed. But I also needed to be concerned about myself. I had no idea what she thought of me. Although I was curious, I did not feel like calling her. Our first meeting had caused me too much stress. I am not a masochist and that is what I would have been if I had gone back for seconds.

There were women all around—young women, old women, ugly women, beautiful women—but I did not feel attracted to any of them. I wasn't able to forget Mayu. Thoughts of her haunted me everywhere—especially during the long monotonous hours of mindless grammar drills with my Language Institute students. April had arrived and with it came spring. The long, persistent winter of this year had finally decided to bid farewell. There was a crispness and warmth in the sunshine, and nascent buds peeked out from the cherry tree branches by the Tidal Basin.

I worked in the Language Institute annex in Rosslyn, Virginia, which housed the Department of Asian and African Languages. I would usually break for lunch at one o'clock and take the skywalk above the city streets to the food court over the Metro station. It certainly didn't have the best food in the world, but it had many stalls with different ethnic foods and one could keep shifting from burritos to souvlaki to Hunan chicken, in hopes of eventually satisfying one's palate.

As I walked down to the food court, I met hordes of people on the skywalk who had been lured outside by the dazzling sun and the spring temperatures. Many had brought their food and were sitting at the outside tables. I bought a gyro and a drink from the Greek stall, and went outdoors to grab a table just being vacated. I sat down on the metal chair and began to nibble the bulging sandwich as gracefully as I could. I could recognize many familiar faces among the passers-by. These outdoor tables lined the portion of the skywalk that connected my annex with the annex where the Institute's administrative offices and the European language departments were housed. I unfolded *The New York Times* and began to read the op-eds. I was halfway through an article questioning the Reagan Administration's policy in Nicaragua when I heard a familiar voice.

"I see you've finished." Mayu was standing over me, blocking the sun.

"Oh, hello," I said. "Are you just arriving for lunch?"

"No. I already ate my sandwich in my classroom. I just came out for some sun and fresh air. It really is a balmy day."

"Then perhaps we can take a walk down toward Iwo Jima Park?" I suggested.

"That sounds good," she said. For the first time, I noticed that she still had a touch of a Finnish accent. We took the stairs down to the street level and threaded our way along the sidewalk in the din of the never-ending traffic on Lynn Street. Men and women, dressed in power suits, hurried by. We walked amidst the soulless Rosslyn high-rises. There was disgust written all over Mayu's face. Her body looked tense and miserable as we walked. I tried to make pleasant small talk to distract her from her moodiness. But my solicitude was of no use until we entered the park and the verdure began to have a softening effect on her.

The chimes of the Netherlands Carillon rang through the noise of the airplanes above and the traffic below. "There certainly is a lot to be said for silence," Mayu said, looking irritably at the traffic and the carillon.

"Noise pollution is the curse of our times," I said. I was immediately embarrassed that I could say something so banal—even if I were desperate for subjects for small talk.

"Noise pollution is a very heavy price to pay for technological advancement," she replied in such a passionate and serious tone that I didn't feel as foolish as I had. I felt as though we were groping toward some common ground. Through some miraculous coincidence, a relative stillness descended on the city as we walked. The Carillon was no longer chiming, no planes were flying, and there was a lull in the traffic. During the entire walk, we had not spoken much. Now we had also fallen silent. It finally seemed as though we were beginning to feel comfortable with each other.

"In Finland, every man has the right of access to nature," she said, wistfully.

"Because there is so *much* nature in Finland."

"There's even more in America," she said. "You people have just lost your knack for seeking it out."

"That's true," I said, momentarily flattered that she counted me among the "you people." "I admire the Finns and their resistance to the 'real world.' I've visited the country."

"When? When?" All of a sudden, Mayu came alive and her impassive face lit up.

"In 1972," I said. "While I was returning from Russia, I took a train from Leningrad to Helsinki and fell in love with Finland."

"How interesting!" she said. The aggressive intellect she had used to keep me off balance from the moment we met seemed to soften.

The moment was spoiled by the chiming of the Carillon. I looked at my watch; I had to be back for the two o'clock class and so did she. We looked at each other, got up and started walking back to work.

"Would you be interested in going out and seeing a play with me at the Source Theater?"

"What's that?" she asked.

"You don't know it?" I asked, surprised. "It's one of the best experimental theaters in Washington."

"Why did you bring that Reagan photo to show me?" she asked, abruptly.

Why, I wondered, won't this woman follow any logical train of thought? "We had met on the street," I said aloud. "I thought if you saw my picture with the President, it would establish my credibility. It was not so much to impress you as to let you know that I was not a dangerous man. I know that women can be leery about men when they first meet them. I just wanted to put you at ease."

Mayu smirked at me. "I had decided not to go out with you again," she said. "But when I discussed it with a friend, she said you sounded interesting and that I should reconsider my decision."

"I appreciate your honesty," I said, thinking that I would have never said anything like that to anyone—no matter how true.

"Besides," Mayu said, with a twinkle in her eye, "a man who loves Finland can't be all bad."

So we made a date in the hallway. "The lions are waiting for a Christian," she said, nodding toward my classroom. I smiled and watched her turn and walk away. Within seconds, her face was lost in thought, as though I had never existed.

****

This was the third consecutive Friday we had gone out. We had dinner at a restaurant in Tyson's Corner. Initially, she had some problems with my choice of restaurant. Apparently, the chain was owned by Nestle, formerly the target of a boycott over its marketing of baby formula in the Third World. The fact that her ex-husband Robert had begun his ascent up the corporate ladder at Nestle didn't help much, either. But the place won her over with its attractive decor, delicious food and good service. In fact, she began raving about the place and the evening was off to a flying start.

We went to see a movie, *The Whales of August*. As we made our way out of the theater, she fell a couple of steps behind me, caught in the press of the crowd. I still heard her make an incisive comment about the theme of the movie we had just seen. Her insight made me turn around and take a second look at her. Driving to her home, we discussed the symbolism of the film. I found myself getting excited, even aroused, by the agility of Mayu's mind.

When we got to her house, the hour was late and her two boys were in bed. Except for the ubiquitous dog, not a soul was stirring. So as not to repeat the events of my first night, I sat down on the good side of the couch. Mayu offered me the usual glass of cloudberry liqueur before taking a seat next to me. I reached over and kissed her. Her thin lips did not stir and her body remained rigid. After a brief pause, she looked at me with narrowed eyes and said, "Finns are slow."

"That surprises me," I said, a little taken aback at her response. "I thought Scandinavian women were known for their openness?"

"Now you know how stereotypes can be misleading," Mayu said coldly and excused herself. She was not gone long. She returned, looking very upset, tears on the brink of flowing from her deep-set eyes. Without uttering a word, she reached for my hand and led me to her bedroom. I certainly wanted to be invited there but not while she was in this frame of mind. I sat down next to her on the edge of the bed, waiting for the mystery of her mood to unfold. Tears were now flowing down her round, flushed cheeks, and her voice was choking. She said, "Colonel Taipali died of a heart attack in Helsinki. Hannu took the message."

For a moment, I felt disoriented, not knowing Colonel Taipali and his connection with Mayu. But then I got thinking—he must have been the current military attaché at the American Embassy in Finland and a former student of Mayu's. "I must call his wife. It must be morning in Finland now," she said, sobbing. Looking down at the message that her son had taken, she picked up the phone to make the international call.

The call did not go through the first time she dialed. It did the second time, but the telephone kept ringing and no one picked up. She replaced the cordless phone into its housing, turned toward me and looked through the mist of her tears straight into my eyes. I embraced her and she yielded. She remained in my arms for quite a while, sobbing. "Why don't you take your suit off and we'll go to bed," she said, undressing.

What an irony of fate. Minutes ago, she was telling me that Finns were slow and now she's asking me to go to bed with her. I had not known Colonel Taipali, so my grief at his sudden and untimely death could only be in a cosmic sense. I could not really feel anything personal. On the other hand, Mayu's proposal to go to bed with her was very real and very personal.

When I returned from the bathroom, dressed only in my underwear, I got under the sheets and discovered that Mayu was completely naked. Our arms found each other's bodies. Soon, it became evident that our needs were very different. Mayu was simply turning to my body for consolation and comfort. I was struggling to balance propriety, compassion and desire. The dam broke and the tide swept over me. When I came to my senses after the storm, Mayu said, "You took advantage of me" in a tone that did not imply an accusation.

"Maybe you needed some diversion to ease the pain?" I suggested, sheepishly.

In spite of all that had happened, she evidently did not feel diverted enough. She began to reminisce about the time she was teaching Finnish to Colonel Taipali. "Since both of his parents were from Finland, he brought a Finnish cultural heritage to class. He had a stoic bearing about him and moved slowly, like a typical Finn. The fact that he grew up on a farm in Wisconsin gave him a rustic exterior that also seemed very Finnish. His wife was Korean. She was pretty, younger, and looked like a dainty little flower. She provided quite a contrast. But it was all deceptive; behind the fragile looks, his wife was made of steel. As anyone who knew the couple soon discovered, she was the one who called the shots. She joined my class later and then often invited me to their home for dinner.

"One Christmastime," Mayu went on, her voice cracking, "we were at the home of Irja Winston, attending a little party. People, mostly Finns, were sitting around the room and someone was singing Finnish Christmas songs. Tears were flowing down the eyes of all the Finns, and Colonel Taipali was crying, too. Well..." Mayu said, almost choking, "you can't get more Finnish than that. And now the man is dead...just like that. He was not much more than 50."

Luminous blue numbers on the clock by the bedside caught Mayu's eye and then mine. It was 5:20. She said, "I'm sorry. I hate to do this to you, but I'm going to have to ask you to leave before my boys wake up."

As Mayu stared from the bed, I got up and put my clothes back on, including my tie. I stealthily walked out of the house. Her street was deserted, and the main road also lacked any real traffic. The hum of the motor and the rhythmic swish of the tires on the road accompanied my thoughts. Who is this woman who is taking a grip on my body and soul, I wondered? I searched for an answer within, as the dawn broke. One by one, the trees, shrubs and neighborhood street-lamps emerged from the darkness like divers surfacing. Perhaps this is the beginning of a new day for me, as well?

CHAPTER FOUR

1958

Several months had passed since Mayu's father had moved out. Over the hoarse coughing of the neighborhood boys experimenting with their first cigarettes, Mayu heard her name being called. The smoke was so thick in the tunnel that she could not clearly see the figure of the person crawling toward her. But she had the hearing of a deer and immediately recognized the voice.

"Oh, my God! It's Mr. Toivonranta," she said. The boys took the cue and put out their cigarettes. The girls stopped giggling, as the smoke cleared. It was the principal of her former school, Lahden Yhteiskoulu, who appeared before them. The older man, on all fours with his tie hanging down, was staring at them in amused bewilderment, as the diffuse autumn light seeped into the tunnel.

"There you are, Mayu. Quite a tunnel you've made here for playing. I would have never found you, if the nurse from your new school, Kansakoulu, hadn't told me where you'd be. Could you interrupt your game, so we can have a chat?"

As the principal's bulky figure backed out of the tunnel, Mayu followed him, dumbfounded. Once on level ground and restored to a posture more usual for *homo sapiens*, the principal told Mayu, "I knew you were no longer at our school, but I had no idea that you'd dropped out because you didn't have the money. Then the nurse from Kansakoulu called me. I was very upset. After all, you were at the top of your class. So I came looking for you."

"Last year," Mayu said heavily, "my mother paid for one semester and my father paid for the other. Now my father has left us, so we can't pay my tuition. That's why I had to go back to public school. My mother is a cleaning woman at the bank and we can barely make it on her salary."

The principal shook his head, while a pained look spread over the broad features of his kind face. The vagaries of human fortune were an endless mystery. "I want you back in my school Monday morning," he said firmly, with a reassuring gesture. Then he turned and left. She kept looking after him as his massive figure disappeared around the corner of the gray stone building.

Mayu remembered how, just a year and a half before, she had taken the entry test for his elite private school, Lahden Yhteiskoulu, without her parent's knowledge. She had been accepted. When she first arrived at the school, she had been awed by the clothes, jewelry and toys that the other children owned. But their materialism and snobbery began to grate on her nerves. The social atmosphere of the school was an affront to her. Yet, she knew that she was more gifted than most of the children in schoolwork, while the teachers had come to recognize and appreciate her. By contrast, when she had returned to Kansakoulu, there had been no school snobbery, but she felt that her mind was being wasted. Without doubt, the education that she was receiving there was inferior.

On Monday morning, as the principal had directed, she returned to Lahden Yhteiskoulu. She approached her homeroom with mixed feelings. When she sat down at her designated seat and opened her desk, she found a pair of sturdy but used brown shoes with a note from one of the teachers. The note read, *Hope these shoes will fit you.*

She felt her face flush with embarrassment. She looked out to the corners of her eyes to see if anyone was watching, then quickly brought down the desk lid. When the hour was over and her classmates were gone, she took the shoes out and put them on. They fit perfectly. She stood by her seat and wriggled her toes, feeling the subtlety of expensive leather all around her feet. But she regarded the shoes ambivalently. After all, somebody else's feet had once occupied their space.

A noise startled her. It was the voice of Miss Bjorklund, her homeroom teacher. She was a tall, thin, middle-aged woman with a slightly pinched expression. "Mayu...welcome back!" she said. "I'm very happy to have you in my class again. Mr. Toivonranta told me and the other teachers that you had dropped out of school.

We were all shocked." She reached out and put a comforting hand on Mayu's shoulder. In a moment, she added, "Here is some money that you can use for school supplies." With gentle insistence, Miss Bjorklund thrust the money into Mayu's hand, then left the room, saying, "Now don't you go away again, dear."

Mayu unfolded the bills and counted. There were eight Marks. She went outside and joined a game of catch with her classmates. She was relieved to see that they were unaware of the charity that she had accepted.

By the time the school day was over, all her teachers had told her how pleased they were that she was back in their school. They could not think of losing such a valuable student. With a broad smile, Mr. Toivonranta assured her that she would not have to pay a single Mark for her education. "As a matter of fact," he said, "you will be doing Lahden Yhteiskoulu a favor by staying."

Several days later, when Mayu was setting out on the walk home, Eila Kunelius, a classmate of hers regarded as the best-dressed girl in school, called to Mayu from the car in which she was being driven home. "Mayu, can you come with me to my house for a short while?"

This invitation from Miss Snobbery puzzled Mayu. During the entire past year, this girl had never deigned to look at her. Mayu stood by the shiny Mercedes for a moment, then asked suspiciously, "Why?"

"I have some clothes I would very much like you to have."

Mayu dropped her eyes and looked at her cotton dress with its floral pattern. She wore it day after day, as it was the only one she had.

"Come on, it won't take long," Eila insisted and opened the front door of her car. The two girls hardly spoke to one another during the short car ride. They soon reached Eila's mansion. Mayu had known that Eila's father was rich, but she had not known just how rich. Eila led Mayu up to her bedroom and dumped a tall pile of clothes in front of her. "There," she said, dismissively.

Mayu hoped that now someone might drive her home, but no one offered. As she walked home, huffing and puffing under the hefty bundle of clothes, she remembered what her father had often said—"Wealth is not properly distributed within this society." Isn't it the truth, she thought. Why should Eila have so many dresses, while I only have one? Her father may be a violent alcoholic, but, she thought, he has the right perspective on the world. As these thoughts crossed her mind, she happened to be passing the odd-looking house where her father lived with Lasse, another drunkard. Maybe I'll go in and visit him some time, she thought, and trudged on.

"Mayu, where have you been?" Raija asked, as Mayu stumbled through the little door, lugging her burden of clothes. "I've been worried to death."

Mayu's only response was to lay the contents of her bundle on the floor. She and her mother examined them and were amazed at the workmanship of the dresses and the quality of their fabric. Though neither was much familiar with these things, they could tell that the dresses were of the latest design. Mayu happily modeled each one for her mother, then hung the dresses up in the closet.

"These will see me through the whole year," she mused.

"I'll iron one of them for you to wear to school tomorrow morning," her mother said.

"Thanks," said Mayu, "But that's not all." She then pulled out the eight Marks and told her mother how she got them. Finally, she showed her mother the shoes that had been part of the day's windfall. They sat down to a meal that Raija had brought home from the bank—leftovers from employee meals.

"I'm glad we didn't run after Dad when he left us," said Mayu. "We're doing all right by ourselves."

Raija told her, "I went to the city welfare office today and told them that you badly needed your teeth looked at. So, I got some money and now you have an appointment to see the dentist tomorrow morning before you go to school."

"It's been an amazing day for us,' said Mayu. One day, she would look back on the irony of such joy at the prospect of going to the dentist. Today, though, she was delighted to experience what the privileged took for granted.

Raija and Mayu fell asleep side by side, thinking that life was not so bad after all.

****

The dentist motioned to Mayu to climb up in the swivel chair. Taking a sharp look at Mayu's clothes, the woman said, "You wear fancy clothes and your mother goes begging for money at the city welfare office for your dental work? Sounds like a scam to me." Before Mayu had a chance to explain how her schoolmate had given her the clothes, the dentist picked up a drill from its cold silver holder in one sudden motion and held it in her hand as if it were a weapon to stab her with.

"This dress was a gift," Mayu managed to say, hoping that the words would be her redemption. But they seemed to annoy the dentist even more.

"You should have worked instead of accepting handouts." She then told Mayu to open her mouth, cutting off any possibility of rebuttal.

When Mayu finally descended from the dentist's chair, her teeth had stopped hurting, but she began to feel another kind of pain. It was the pain of humiliation and it refused to go away. If people need help, it should be given to them without shaming them, she told herself. If my mother and I are poor, it's not our fault. We are not lazy and we are doing what we are supposed to do. She walked from the dentist to school, still smarting. Even as wrapped up as she was in her thoughts, Mayu noticed that people were looking at her differently today than they usually did. She could see that they admired how well-dressed she looked now.

Quietly, Mayu entered her classroom and sat down in her seat. When she looked around, she saw Eila whispering something in the ear of another rich girl sitting next to her. When they both looked at her, Mayu was sure that they were mocking her. By the time school ended, the whole class knew that she was wearing Eila's cast-offs. If she could have, she would have ripped the dress off and thrown it in Eila's face. Paranoia set in and she felt that the whole school—even the whole world—was laughing at her.

****

It was an odd-looking house—rectangular, decrepit, giving the impression of an oversized antique matchbox. It always stared at her on her way to and from school, arousing conflicting feelings in her heart. Maybe I should go in and see my father? Mayu thought. It's Friday and he should be home by now. The door with its peeling gray paint yielded to her touch and opened to reveal a disheveled man drinking on a couch, surrounded by empty beer cans and whiskey bottles.

This is my father's brother-in-law, she thought. Or, I should say, he was, until he deserted his wife, just like my father. "Hello," she said, keeping one foot outside and holding the door open with one hand.

"Who are you?" he asked, feebly. A coughing fit followed.

"I'm Aarne's daughter," she answered.

"Oh, you're Mayu," he said. He pointed to the right with the open bottle in his hand, sloshing the liquor: "He's in there."

Mayu stepped inside the house, walking over and around the cases and bottles as though they were landmines. The door was ajar. As she went in, she was startled to find her father in bed. And he was not alone. She felt a thick nausea in her stomach. As she turned around and was about to leave, her father yelled: "What's the matter, Mayu? Haven't you ever seen a whore before?"

Mayu froze, her eyes glazed over. She was looking at nothing, but she heard the woman climb off the bed and quickly pull on her clothes. The smell of sex trailed behind, as the woman slipped out the door. Then Mayu was alone with her father. This was not the first time Mayu had seen her father in bed with a woman, but that woman had always been her mother. It was shattering to find him with some other woman—worse, with a prostitute. Prostitutes don't go around popping into men's beds for pleasure, she thought. I'm sure they have to be hired. So, her father was clearly the guilty party in this whole affair. She shook her head and her stomach heaved at the thought that his body had just been mixing with the body of a whore. She thought of her long-suffering mother and tears welled up in her eyes. When her eyes could focus again, she saw her own reflection stare back at her from the mirror above her father's bed. There was an uncanny resemblance between her own face and her father's. Her father was finished dressing now. He caught her eye and she decided not to look away.

"Lasse inherited a chunk of money from an old aunt who croaked. Now, we are both enjoying the money the way we know best…with wine, women and song."

Her father asked her to sit down. There was no chair in the room and she was loath to sit on the bed where that woman had just been. She remained standing in the doorway. She told her father that she was back in Lahden Yhteiskoulu and explained the humiliating experiences she'd had at the dentist and at school.

"They have all come from the same hairy place…and even the queen farts," was his response. He settled down on the bed. Then, staring into space, his voice took on a prophetic tone, as he began, "Communism is one political philosophy which has done away with all social snobbery." As he talked about the noble ideas, his words brought about a thaw in Mayu's feelings. She knew that he had earned the right to talk about communism. He had put his own life on the line during the Finnish civil war in 1917, smuggling food to Red inmates in a prison camp. She also knew that all of the communist captives were eventually shot dead by their captors and dumped in mass graves. My father's bitterness, she thought, must have stemmed in part from this grisly part of his and his nation's history.

It struck her how much they were alike—not only physically, she thought, but also in our thinking. Every time he was sober and they sat down to talk, she would feel such harmony with his outlook that other things didn't seem to matter. He had a chameleon-like quality. One moment he was threatening her mother and taunting Mayu with a prostitute in his bed, and the next moment he was enthralling her with his ideas and philosophy. With him, she never knew which way it would be.

"What is life like under communism?" she asked.

"Think of a water faucet in a public place. People who need water come to it, turn it on and get as much water as they need. Then they return home and nobody looks down on them for their act. Isn't it wonderful?"

"Yes, it is, if the water faucet is for everybody and some people don't have more rights over it than others," Mayu responded.

"Think of a faucet from which people could get other things they need…clothes, for instance."

"Oh! That would be such a wonderful thing," she said, very animated.

"In communism, the state or the society is that faucet where people can get what they need. And nobody can hog too much, or run the risk of receiving too little. Because of this egalitarianism, there is no room for snobbery, or people who puff themselves up while they deflate others."

"That is what I really like," said Mayu, with conviction. "Maybe I should join the Communist Youth Group when I'm a little older, so I can work toward bringing communism to Finland?"

"Bringing communism to Finland would be fine. But I'm not sure about you joining youth groups, or girl scouts, or things like that."

"Why not?"

"Because then you have to wear a uniform. And uniforms suggest blind obedience to authority. I don't like that. You should never have to salute somebody on cue. I want you always to question what's said to you—especially when the words sound clever, because that's when they're most dangerous.'

Mayu ran over and threw her arms around her father. "I love the way your mind works, Dad! But how come you do such terrible things? You treated my mother like dirt, you left us and now you're living here with Lasse as a drunk."

Her father thought for a moment, thumped his breast with mock melancholy and said, "I have a stone here where most folks have a heart."

"I should be getting home," Mayu said, quietly. "Mom will be worried." Subdued now, she headed for the door. As usual, her father offered her a little money—to assuage his conscience for not supporting us, she thought—but he had to press it on her twice before she took it from his hand. On Mayu's way out, she heard

Lasse grunt something. Trying to decipher what he was saying, she tripped and started an avalanche of liquor bottles. The rumble haunted her long after she had left the ramshackle house.

"All liquor and no heart," she kept saying to herself over and over again, as she hurried toward her mother's bank. Raija was startled to see her flushed face and tear-swollen eyes. As Mayu hugged her mother, she was afraid that she might contaminate her with the filth that she had picked up from her father's world of communism, whores and liquor. "I went to see my Dad and I just got so upset." As she spoke, tears rolled down her cheeks and she clenched her teeth in anger.

"I see," Raija said. "You know your Dad, so why should the way he acts surprise or upset you anymore? I would have thought it would be old hat by now."

"He says that he has a stone for a heart. How did he get like that?"

"It's a long story, Mayu. He lost his parents when he was six and went to work in other people's homes. Growing up, he never knew what love was."

"That must have been horrible. Maybe that's why he can't give me the real love a father should give his child? But it still hurts. He was in bed with a whore when I went to see him."

Raija winced at Mayu's frankness. "Your father is a very troubled man, Mayu." Raija wiped away Mayu's tears with her kind, calloused hand and kissed her on the cheek. "Let's do something about your face. You can't be seen like this in public."

Raija didn't have any make-up and would not have known how to use it, even if she did. Guided by her country instincts, she went to the bank cafeteria kitchen, took a package of flour down from the shelf and poured a little bit into her open hand. She powdered Mayu's face with the flour to tone down her ruddiness. After tidying up a little and packing up the cafeteria's leftover food, mother and daughter left the bank.

The first thing Mayu did when they came home was to get all the clothes Eila had given her out of the closet. "Don't you want to eat first?" Raija asked. "Then you can admire those fancy clothes all evening." Mayu did not respond to her mother. Instead, she picked up a dress and cast it into the fireplace.

"What on earth are you doing? Are you out of your mind?"

"No, actually I've come to my senses. My Dad has always told me not to forget where I come from. When I wear these clothes, I am denying my humble origins and turning myself into a laughing-stock. It's not really good for me."

"You give me such grown-up talk. It's frightening. Why can't you be a normal little girl?"

Mayu didn't take her eyes off the dress, which smoldered a little, sputtering out flashes of blue and red before bursting into flame. She threw in another dress, which was soon engulfed. Mayu watched the destruction with fierce pleasure on her face. Except for a few specks of flour, her face was so red that it seemed to be molded out of coagulated blood, as though the sculptor had forgotten to put skin on. The flame-light was reflected on her livid face, creating a weird effect. Her frown deepened and her expression was intense. When the second dress was reduced to ashes, Mayu said, "Mom, I want to tell you a story I read in a magazine at school."

Mayu told her mother the story of the town mouse and the country mouse. The town mouse scorned the simple, quiet life of his country cousin. The country mouse accepted the town mouse's invitation to visit. The food and surroundings were indeed sumptuous, but the visit ended tragically; the town mouse was devoured by a dog in the midst of the feasting. "The moral of the story," Mayu said, "is that a life of peace and poverty is better than a life of wealth with indignity and fear."

"That's an interesting story," said Raija.

"Yes. You see now? I don't want to wear pretty clothes and be insulted each day at school. I'll be happy to wear one dress and feel good about myself."

Raija walked over and hugged Mayu, then joined her in burning the symbols of her humiliation. "You sound so grown-up and know such big, big words," said Raija. For a moment, it was almost as if she were the child and Mayu was the mother. Standing together, they watched the last dress burn down to ashes. The simplicity of Mayu's gesture brought a smug feeling of righteousness with it. The two basked in the illusion—convinced that even though they were poor, they were somehow better than the rich.

Late that night, Raija was nearly asleep while Mayu lay wide awake, haunted by the thought that her father didn't love her. Her mother was loving and devoted—although as Mayu secretly knew, not very intelligent. Mayu couldn't talk with her the way that she could with her father. But Raija's love more than compensated for her other shortcomings. Mayu felt that her mother was there just for her. *But my father?* Doesn't he feel any love for me at all? After all, I look like him and think like him. There should have been a special bond between us, but there is none.

In spite of her mother's explanation that her father had grown up without love, this bothered her. What, she wondered impatiently, did having been loved have to do with being able to love? They are two totally different things, aren't they? Perhaps men cannot love like women? Though she had a brother, Heikki, she had never really known a brother's love. He was 13 years older than she was and had left home to join the army when she was five. And twelve years with her father was an uneasy existence, a wasp's nest of tension, stirring up confusion about love in her heart.

"Your father never wanted to have children," Raija said, drifting out of sleep.

"I didn't know that. So Heikki and I are unwanted?" Mayu felt her mind go blank with shock.

"I was able to have Heikki because Aarne was in prison. Aarne and his brother decided to go to the Soviet Union illegally on foot. They got lost on the Finnish-Soviet border. After they went around and around, they were picked up by the Finnish border patrol and put into jail. I was already pregnant with Heikki when that happened, but Aarne didn't know. He was furious when he got out of jail and found out that he had a son. After that, he forced me to abort two pregnancies. The country woman who did the second one used a knitting needle. I developed an infection and almost died.

"When I was pregnant with you, Mayu, I just plain refused to have another abortion. So your father put me on a toboggan, pushed me to the middle of a frozen lake, dug a hole through the ice and stuck my legs into the icy water. I felt like I was going to die. My legs turned blue with cold. But still I refused to abort and finally, he decided to give up."

Mayu was flabbergasted to hear this story. She clung to her mother, as she had not done since she was a baby. The warmth of her mother's body against her face comforted her and helped to ease the pain. If my father had had his way, I would have never been born.

****

The neighborhood children were out in full force with their toboggans. A soft snow had fallen the night before, giving the drab town an illusory look of peace and beauty. Mayu suggested that they play her favorite sledding game and link all the toboggans into a train. The train was going full speed when a car entered the alley and the two vehicles nearly collided. The driver of the car skidded to a stop, while the train careened into a wall, spilling all the sledders into the snow. Fortunately, no one was hurt. While climbing from the wreckage of her game, Mayu felt a tap on her shoulder.

"Heikki!" she shouted when she recognized her brother. She tried to embrace him, but he remained stiffly impassive. Heikki was a tall, beefy young man with blonde hair and thin lips that always seemed just short of a sneer.

"Mayu, wash my car," he said, coolly. "I'll give you 50 pennies."

"So it was your car that nearly hit us? Are you bringing the car from Sweden?"

"Yes. Now get on with cleaning it," Heikki said, without looking at his little sister. He walked toward the apartment. Mayu looked at the car. It was all splattered with mud and slush.

"I need to get a bucket," Mayu said excitedly, and followed him up to the apartment.

Without saying a word to his mother, Heikki loosened the string of a duffle bag and dumped the contents on the table.

"Bananas!" Mayu shouted from the entrance of the apartment. She ran and picked up the bunch.

"Heikki!" Raija came up to him and hugged him as he stood immobile, his lips smirking.

"Go ahead, eat them," he said to Mayu. But she didn't move. She had never eaten a banana or even seen one, except in picture books. Heikki broke a banana from the bunch, peeled it halfway down and handed it to Mayu. "Now eat up," he ordered her.

Mayu bit into the luscious fruit and, after the strange initial sensation on her taste buds, decided that she liked it. She gobbled up the banana and then stood there holding the peel, wondering if her brother had instructions on how it was to be disposed of, since he seemed to know everything else.

"Run along now and clean my car till it shines," he said, gesturing for her to go. Then, he turned to his mother. As Mayu dropped the banana peel in the trash bin and picked up a bucket and sponge, she heard Heikki speak to her mother, "Sinikka and I are planning to get married and this apartment will suit us to a tee. I'd like you and Mayu to leave."

"We could do that," Mayu heard her mother respond meekly. Mayu left the apartment, wondering why her mother always bowed to other people's whims. She lugged bucket after bucket of water from the landlord's faucet and carefully sponged the car clean. Then she could read the letters: *Saab*. There were some bumps and dents and rusted spots, so it must have been a used car. But it didn't look bad, as the dirt was washed away. Mayu took one last look of satisfaction at the machine. Now that she was finished, she thought she would go up and visit the brother she had not seen since he had gone to work in Sweden. As she turned around, swinging the bucket in her hand, she found herself face-to-face with him. He thrust 50 pennies into her hand, got in the car and drove away, screeching the wheels on the thin ice. The car turned off the alley on to the main street and disappeared. Mayu looked down at the coins that Heikki had put in her hand. The only thing he gives is money, she thought sadly, and tears welled in her eyes.

****

It was Mayu's thirteenth birthday. When she awoke, she didn't expect this to be different from any other birthday she had marked. Sure, her mother had baked birthday cakes from ingredients that she'd brought home from the bank kitchen and she had blown out one more candle each year. But somehow, birthdays never seemed significant to her.

What's the big deal? Mayu thought. Except that each year, one gets a year older. Why the fuss? Birthdays don't bring the realization of the aspirations and dreams of a year, anyway. So why bother? Though her precocious mind was so used to exploring cosmic issues, this morning she thought along more concrete, pedestrian lines. Will my birthday bring a new dress or a pair of shoes, or will there be just enough money to buy milk for the week?

Raija took Mayu in her arms, kissed her on the forehead and wished her a happy birthday. To Mayu, it felt good, though it didn't feel different from any other day. She received this diet of love from her mother on a regular basis. In fact, she almost took it for granted.

"We are going to the market," Raija announced. Mayu was surprised, but she chose not to question her mother, knowing that it would be futile. When Raija wanted to keep a secret, her lips were sealed.

Mayu was incredulous when they entered a bicycle shop and her mother began to price different bikes. This isn't happening! she thought. The very solicitous salesman expounded the virtues of the best brands the shop had. Mayu listened, though she knew that all the bikes he was describing were prohibitive.

"Let's see which one Mayu likes," said Raija, smiling with shy pride at her daughter.

If this is all a dream, Mayu thought, I might as well make my contribution. She pointed to a pink lady's bike with a blue and pink striped crossbar. "I like this one," she said, tentatively.

"How much?" her mother asked the salesman.

"Two hundred and thirty Marks," he responded. "It's a real steal."

"We'll take it," Raija said.

When they emerged from the store, Mayu was in a stupor. Raija's monthly pay was 170 Marks and she had just spent 230 for a bicycle for her daughter! Mayu didn't know whether to be happy or unhappy, excited or depressed. She remembered a time when she and her mother had had no money at all, not even to buy milk, so they had gone to her father's house with a wheelbarrow and collected all the liquor bottles and sold them for five pennies apiece.

So where did the 230 Marks come from? Her mother must have done extra work, denied herself the things she needed, or just taken out a loan which would take her forever to repay. In any case, her mother's act drove home her mother's real valor. Never again, she vowed, will I take my mother for granted. Love, caring and sacrifice are noble qualities. She turned and hugged her mother for a long time. Then she mounted the bike and rode very carefully. This was not just a piece of machinery. It was a piece of her mother's heart.

****

Mayu's thirteenth birthday brought her unprecedented joy in the form of a bicycle. It also brought, more than ever, the realization that one of her breasts was not growing. She could look around her school and watch the breasts of girls her age becoming well-developed. One of hers, too, was becoming shapely and round. The other one, however, remained as flat as ever. She saw how boys, especially the older ones, looked at girls' breasts, and she realized how important they were in men's eyes. When she mentioned her concern to her mother, Raija said something unhelpful like, "It's your father's curse." Although Mayu didn't understand what that meant, she didn't bother to ask for an explanation.

Mayu's new bike gave her mobility, but it also made her more conspicuous. Because of her lack of physical development, her rides around the neighborhood which should have been exhilarating became embarrassing. Every time she climbed on her bike, she felt like her flawed body was on display, with everyone staring at her. With the passage of each day, that feeling became even more intense. There were mysterious changes taking place within her. She wanted boys to notice her and be attracted to her. She wanted to be with them. Yet she didn't feel comfortable among them.

She met an older boy named Bo-Erik, who also had a bicycle. The two of them rode everywhere together. One day, he said to her, "Come. I want to show you my house."

She liked him and was curious about him, so she followed him to his house. His parents weren't home. Bo-Erik took her hand and led her into the sauna. He kissed her over and over in the dim, humid room, panting with passion and impatience. He undid the buttons of her dress with trembling fingers and slid it off her shoulder. Suddenly, he stopped dead and his face froze in an expression of shock and revulsion. "Oh, God! You only have one breast!" he blurted, accusingly.

Mayu ran out of the sauna, pulling her dress back on. She pedaled home blindly, sobbing with frustration and humiliation. Why is it that I want boys to notice me? Safer to keep them at bay, she thought. She found comfort instead in the companionship of her bicycle. It gave her freedom, took her places and never hurt her with shallow judgments.

CHAPTER FIVE

1969

On the long flight from Helsinki to New York, Mayu never stopped crying. The Pan Am stewardesses were very concerned at first and continued to ask if they could do anything to help. Mayu only stopped long enough to ask for Kleenex. Eino had driven her to the airport. During the month preceding her departure, they were getting along better than they had in a long time. They had both found themselves working on the same project, studying the impact of television viewing on young people, and it had brought them closer together. Meanwhile, the other men in Mayu's life had drifted off, one after the other.

Richard Taki, the Tanzanian student at Patrice Lumumba University with whom she had fallen head over heels in love during the conference in Sofia, had driven a wedge between Mayu and Eino for a time. After her return to Finland, she had written passionate letters to Richard. He responded to her second letter with an invitation to come and see him in Moscow.

When she got there, they could not, of course, be together in his dormitory room, and she could not take him to her hotel. When Russians saw a white woman with a black man, they reacted very negatively, yelling epithets at her and calling her a whore, so Mayu was afraid to go out in public with him. The couple met instead at the house of an African diplomat. Their unions were as electrifying now as the first one in the park in Sofia had been. Mayu's hunger for Richard took her to the Soviet Union 19 times in one year and never once did she question her obsession.

When their relationship reached a certain point, Richard said, "I will take you to Africa, introduce you to my parents and we'll get married."

Mayu had not foreseen his proposal. She found that she was dismayed. Having a passionate love affair with an African man in Europe was one thing, but to make a life in Africa with him was an entirely different matter. After agonizing for several days, she had to say no.

Richard's reaction shocked Mayu. After letters flew back and forth between Helsinki and Moscow, Mayu arrived in Moscow and called Richard at the dorm. His roommate answered and, after a few moments during which Mayu could hear muffled voices, the roommate came back on the line and said apologetically, "He refuses to come to the phone. He says he doesn't want to talk to you."

Mayu knew why he was behaving this way, but the absoluteness of it was incomprehensible to her. It was a very painful moment for her, but her pride prevented her from chasing him any further.

Mayu had met Richard through Thomas, who was also at the University, but she and Richard had never told him the nature of their affair, nor contacted him when Mayu was in Moscow. She called him now. He was surprised and delighted that she was in town. "You should have written to me! If I had known you were coming, I would have been better prepared to receive you," he said in his characteristic jovial way. Thomas's company temporarily eased Mayu's heartbreak, but getting over Richard was slow and heavy going.

While Richard had never come to see her in Finland, Thomas said he would. In fact, he did show up at the beginning of summer when she was in Lahti visiting her mother.

At first, her mother felt some apprehension about her daughter going out with an African man, her imagination running wild with visions of her precious Mayu running around Africa with a bunch of half-naked cannibals. "But we're only friends," Mayu assured her. But Raija could not resist wondering what kind of children would come from such a union.

Mayu introduced Thomas to many of her friends and relatives, and they were all charmed by his geniality. Her brother, Heikki, took him to the sauna and the two men sat there naked on the cedar benches and discussed Ghanaian politics, with more gestures than words. On the street, children were fascinated by

Thomas and would walk up to Mayu and ask her if his curly hair were real.

One evening, after they had all been to a restaurant, Mayu's mother walked along, supporting herself on Thomas's shoulder. In Finnish, she said to Mayu, "I wouldn't mind being mother-in-law to this young man." Mayu laughed at her change of heart, but didn't translate this remark for Thomas.

At the end of his visit, Thomas surprised Mayu by proposing, just as her mother had foreseen.

"You must be joking, Thomas," she said. "I thought we were just friends?"

"No, I'm not joking. I want to take you to Ghana with me at the end of my studies," he said, a very serious expression on his artless features.

"Ghana…as in Africa?" she asked in the bantering tone they usually used together. Thomas laughed mirthlessly. She went on, "First of all, I don't see you in that light. I don't love you and I can't see myself marrying anybody I don't love. And even if I did love you, the cross-cultural problems of making my life in Africa would be so enormous that our marriage wouldn't survive the pressure."

Thomas was crushed. He didn't say much for the remainder of his visit. Nothing Mayu could do cheered him up. He finally packed his bags and left Finland by train in the same blue mood. He wrote a cool letter from Moscow to say, *It would be best if we didn't see each other or communicate anymore.*

The pain she felt on this separation was much less than it had been with Richard. Mayu thought, however, that she had discovered a truth. To Africans, it seemed, it had to be all or nothing between men and women. Finnish couples could remain friends, even if one of them ruled out the possibility of marriage. She thought, apparently for Africans these gray areas do not exist.

There was one more marriage proposal, from yet another continent. Actually, it came from Sri Lanka. Mayu received a one-way ticket from Helsinki to Colombo in the mail, with a marriage proposal in antiquated, flowery English. As she read the letter, she could picture the huge round face of the Trotskyite Buddhist monk, Vajirabuddhi, in her mind. She smiled, as she remembered his hapless wooing. He had done everything wrong, and now he had gone and done it again. She thought of how much the ticket must have cost him and how deluded he had been to buy it. She returned the ticket, along with a note, reading, *Thanks for the thought, but East will have to remain East and West will have to remain West. Never shall the twain meet in this lifetime.* She had second thoughts about the way she'd worded her response, but never about the response itself.

Mayu was possessed with a fierce desire to get on with her life. Thoughts of home-grown Eino seeped into the vacuum, as thoughts of these exotic men faded and became less compelling.

At this time, both Mayu and Eino were traveling all over the country on their television project—sometimes together and sometimes separately. Their paths often crossed, as they mixed with young people and secretly observed their reactions to television. Then Mayu and Eino worked on the final report, which threw them together for long hours at a time. The famous journalism professor, Kaarle Noordenstring, the sponsor of the project, liked their work. The final report was submitted to Magyar Radio and Television OY as an exemplary piece of research.

While they were researching, Mayu and Eino found out a lot about the young people, some of whom were experimenting with drugs and sexual liberty in those heady days of the late 60's. But they also made some discoveries about each other. Eino was obsessive, compulsive and pathologically neat, while Mayu was intellectual, disorganized and opinionated. Yet they also found that they could live and work together.

Over the previous five years of their on-again, off-again relationship, Eino had repeatedly told Mayu that she needed to find out what she wanted for herself. And she had certainly tried. But she had returned to him after each affair and he had remained an enduring element in her life. Mayu thought that her need for Eino was linked to her great need for security. Although she never fell in love with him—in fact she often found it hard to love him—she needed him as one might need a roadmap in an unfamiliar country. His was the first positive male influence she had known in her life.

Hey, this might even work, Mayu finally said to herself. Eino never stopped saying, "Sex is for procreation only." He would feel guilty each time they made love. But as they would lie in bed afterwards, there was genuine affection between them. She had come to feel a lot closer to him.

Mayu's outstanding academic work earned her a Fulbright scholarship, an unusual one that offered her a choice between studying in the Soviet Union or the United States. Because of her renewed feeling for Eino, she was not as elated with the scholarship as she would have been if she had been alone in the world. An inner voice told her to take the scholarship and run; to get away from the false feelings she had developed for Eino. But there was still a tie there. And if she did go abroad, which direction would it be? East or West? The education minister told her that she should go to the United States. It would always be possible to go to the Soviet Union later. But if she went to the USSR now, Americans would not accept her later.

In the end, American paranoia about the Soviet Union influenced her decision. She announced her choice to friends and family. For her mother, it was a moment of pride. For her brother, it was a moment of grief. His sister was going to the land of the capitalists where Nixon had recently come to power. Eino greeted the news with graceful resignation. At last, he thought, Mayu will be doing what she really wants to do.

In spite of the insistent inner voice, Mayu felt ambivalent about leaving. As her plane left Helsinki, Mayu was overwhelmed with sadness. Even when the captain announced the final approach to JFK, she couldn't shake off her gloomy mood. She changed planes and heading for Minnesota.

Mayu arrived in Minneapolis at 3:00 in the morning; the runways were just being reopened after a fierce snowstorm. At that hour, she didn't expect to be met. Surely, my host won't still be waiting after such a long delay. She drifted through the terminal, wondering what to do next.

Suddenly, a tall, thin man appeared. "Are you Mayu Kaariainen?" he asked.

She was startled and embarrassed. Her eyes were swollen and her face was fuzzy with exhaustion. She was also wearing blue jeans and a baggy sweater, and didn't want to be seen by anyone—particularly not by someone with whom she was going to work. But he, too, was untidy—his blonde hair disheveled, his clothes crumpled. He wore an intense expression on his youthful face.

"How did you recognize me?"

"It wasn't hard to spot a lost Finnish gal. By the way, I'm Jerry Summers."

"I guessed as much. You're going to be my advisor. But I didn't expect you to be so young."

"I apologize for my youth," the young man said, with a mild ironic smile. "I'll try to compensate for it by acting more mature."

Mayu laughed. She felt her tension dissipate in a surge of warmth for the man. After his car's wheels spun in place for a moment, the vehicle took off, the snow beneath the tires muffling the sound of cracking ice.

"I'm sorry you had to wait for me so long," Mayu said. "The weather delayed the flight."

"No problem. It's just that I was worried about you."

They were both tired and Mayu could hardly keep her puffy eyes open. Still, she tried to keep up a conversation, as Jerry negotiated his Buick over the treacherous streets. Snow was falling again, but not heavily this time. Small flurries floated down and the windshield wipers quickly cleared them. The car came to a stop in front of a two-story house that appeared in the darkness to be a duplex.

"Alice and the kids are asleep, so we'd better try to be quiet." For the first time, Mayu realized that Jerry was married. Talking in whispers, he led her upstairs to a small bedroom, put her bags down on the bed and closed the door. "You can stay here till tomorrow. No, I should say till later today. Then you can move into the university dorm." He bent over and kissed her. She felt the unmistakable jolt of sexuality in his kiss. After he left the room, Mayu dropped on the bed and went to sleep, thinking about Jerry's kiss. Thoughts of Eino were conveniently shoved into the background.

****

Her first impression of the University of Minnesota was that it was huge. Minneapolis was also a far cry from the small university town of Jyvaskyla where she had spent the past five years. But she found that she could create a small, manageable world of her own—a sort of campus within a campus—that took away the feeling of solitude that a large, impersonal state university could inflict on its students.

Jerry Summers certainly helped. He was in the habit of helping all female students, especially the Fulbright scholars, by taking more than just a professional interest in them. He and Professor Noordenstring had been in touch, so Jerry knew about the project Mayu had been involved in—the effects of the electronic media on the human mind. Mayu's Fulbright work was to be a continuation of her Finnish study. It was Summers's job to guide her research using American subjects. He decided to incorporate the information Mayu needed in a graduate seminar that he was teaching to a group of five students.

During the class, as Mayu was reporting on the work she had done in Finland, a tall, good-looking student with long blond hair and blue eyes burst into the room. He dumped his books on the desk with a bang and, tossing his hair, sat down and said, "Sorry I'm late."

Mayu continued after the interruption, but kept stealing glances at the handsome, insouciant latecomer. At the end of class, she walked out with some other students with whom she had made a lunch date. They had walked only a few steps when the tardy young man came up from behind and said, "I once knew a professor who taught in Finland."

It was a good line to attract Mayu's attention, but as the conversation progressed, she noticed that he didn't seem to know much about the professor or Finland. So, they ended up talking about each other's programs and discovered that they had one more course in common—*Sociology of Adolescence.*

"My name is Robert," he said, walking off. "See you whenever."

When the *Sociology of Adolescence* class began on Thursday morning, Robert sat next to Mayu and asked her if she would have dinner with him that evening. She had no engagements and, since the semester was just starting, there was no homework. She accepted.

Robert told her that he lived in a one-bedroom apartment provided by the university. She imagined a tiny one-room space like the one she had lived in as a girl. When she walked in, she realized that it was actually a three-room apartment with a living-room, kitchen and bedroom. What he had done with the apartment impressed her. The furniture was modern and functional. It had come with the apartment, so he hadn't chosen the style. But he had put his own tasteful personal stamp on the living space, with Picasso and Chagall posters on the walls and a bowl of tropical fruit on the table.

Robert cooked spaghetti. As they sat down to wrap the elusive pasta around their forks, they talked animatedly. Mayu noticed how easy it was to talk to him. At one point, it seemed that their cultural and language differences fell by the wayside. They began to finish each other's sentences. Finally, they fell into companionable silence. On the couch where they sat, Robert put his head on Mayu's lap and fell asleep.

Not long ago, I met this creature, Mayu thought to herself. It's amazing just how fast he has insinuated himself into my life. She felt a spark of sexual interest in him, but even more so, she felt maternally protective toward him. She kept very still and let him sleep. It was late in the night when he awoke.

"It's late," he said, yawning and looking at his watch. "I should drive you to your apartment."

Early that morning, back in her room, Mayu fell asleep thinking of Robert and how comfortable he had made her feel. She appreciated that he had not pressured her for sex. And with what ease he had fallen asleep in her lap! Seeing things in absolutes as Mayu always did, she found him sensuous and very lovable. She hoped he would call to ask her out again. The telephone woke her. She picked up the receiver.

"Hello?"

"Mayu, this is Robert. I hope I didn't wake you up."

"Yes, you did. But I don't mind. Not if it's you. I should have been getting up anyway."

"I'm sorry about being so tired and falling asleep on you last night. I want to make up for it. Maybe we could meet again tonight and go to see a movie or something?"

"What's the time?"

"You mean, the show?"

"No, now."

"11:00," he said.

"What about the show?"

"7:30."

"I'd like that," said Mayu. "It would be a good way to spend a Saturday evening. What time do you want to meet?"

"Why don't we just show up at the movie house when we feel like it and see if we have ESP enough to get there at the same time," Robert said, with laughter in his voice.

"Very funny," said Mayu.

"Okay, okay. Why don't I pick you up around 6:00? We'll go early. It'll give us a chance to spend some time together."

"Fine. See you at 6:00."

When they arrived at the movie theater that evening to see *Dr. Zhivago,* it surprised Robert that Mayu insisted on going Dutch.

"Finnish women are very liberated," she informed him. The love scenes in the movie inspired them to touch and explore each other in the darkness of the theater. When the movie ended, they were anxious to be alone, so they rushed back to Robert's apartment. Leaving a trail of clothes behind, they ended up on the bed. At the very last moment, Mayu remembered to use the foam she carried with her in her pocketbook for just such an occasion. They made love passionately.

"You're a very unusual woman. I've never known anybody like you," Robert told her, as he lay next to her, still panting. Mayu squeezed his hand. He added, "I don't think I'm going to let you go back to Finland."

"But my Fulbright stipulates that I return," she said. Her tone implied that she was not anxious to go back.

"My parents are ultra-conservative Republicans," Robert said. "They worked and voted for Barry Goldwater in '64. I never thought in my wildest dreams that I would be falling for the daughter of a Finnish communist."

"And when I came to the U.S.," she countered, "I didn't think that I would be falling for anybody at all."

"Do you want to move in with me, Mayu?"

Mayu burst out laughing and said, "That's taking things a little too fast. We've had a couple of good dates and the sex was great, but I don't see making whole life changes on the basis of such transient pleasures."

"I've had something like 200 women, but I've never known anybody like you. You're so intellectually stimulating that in the short time I've known you, I find myself completely absorbed by you."

"Hold on, Robert. If I were you, I'd watch to make sure I didn't exaggerate my feelings. What you feel may be momentary and transitory. When you get up tomorrow morning and see the light of day, you may feel differently."

He looked at her closely and rendered his assessment: "You're a pessimist."

"No. That's what I call realism, Robert. Sometimes, our own feelings betray us. But I believe you mean what you say sincerely; I'm not questioning your motives."

Robert did not say anything. He had begun to doze off. She kissed him and held him in her arms. Long after he had fallen asleep, she stayed awake thinking. But she wasn't able to reach any conclusion about this enigma called Robert.

****

Mayu's period was late. Despite her precautions, she was sure that she was pregnant. Her heart and mind ached with uncertainty. She didn't consider having an abortion because of her mother's horrible experiences. But how will Robert react to this news, she wondered. Will he want to marry me? If he doesn't, what will I do with the child? Motherhood would totally ruin her own plans for her life—like getting her doctorate. And she couldn't see raising her child out of wedlock. The baby needed a father. How she had missed the presence of a loving father in her own childhood! On the other hand, she barely knew Robert and, as she had told him, it was too soon to know if they would make a good couple or not.

With these thoughts filling her mind, she walked toward the campus library. On the sidewalk, she ran into David Howard, a fellow student whom she had come to like and with whom she had shared many bracing intellectual conversations.

"Where've you been keeping yourself, Mayu? I hardly see you anymore."

Mayu told him that things had moved very fast between her and Robert, and that she suspected that she was pregnant.

"Oh, God!" said David, his face showing confusion and concern. Reluctantly, he told Mayu that he had just seen Robert kissing a university girl named Cynthia. This news upset Mayu so much that she abruptly left David. She went back to her apartment and closed herself in her bedroom.

At first, she was not so much angry at Robert as she was with herself for the way she was reacting to what she had heard. Again and again, she played back in her mind what she had already told Robert: a few dates and a few good sexual encounters do not add up to a life-long commitment. What's more, the very casualness of their affair didn't give Mayu the right to expect Robert's undivided attention. But then she broke down and beat the walls bitterly. With ruddy face, swollen eyes and disheveled hair, she went to see her advisor.

"What's the matter with you?" Jerry Summers asked, with concern. There was no point in hiding the truth from him, so Mayu poured out the whole story. Summers closed the door. "Go to the Student Health Center and they will tell you for sure if you are pregnant," he said, consolingly. As she was about to go to the door, he kissed her on the lips.

Mayu had misgivings about Jerry Summers's kisses. Still, they tasted sweet and she did feel comforted, as she came out of Summers's office. While she was waiting for the results of her pregnancy test, her period came in a heavy flow of blood. Though she was deeply relieved, her heart was not easy. She was filled with jealousy over the matter of Cynthia.

The next time Mayu and Robert met, she decided not to say anything about what she had heard from David Howard. When they began to make love, Mayu knew there was something wrong. She knew what was bothering her—but what was the matter with Robert? At first, he had difficulty getting an erection. Finally, when he attained some semblance of it, he couldn't reach a climax.

"Maybe we ought to stop and talk it over," Mayu suggested. Robert looked relieved. She got up to make some coffee.

"I don't know how to put it, Mayu, without being offensive."

"What do you mean?" asked Mayu, fearing the worst. "Come right out and say what you mean."

"It's your weight—it would be helpful if you lost some."

"And how do you suggest I do that?"

"If you go to the Medical Center," Robert said, "they might put you on a diet regimen."

"I'll see what I can do," Mayu responded weakly, sounding like her mother. To her surprise, Robert abruptly got up and began to get dressed. "What's going on?" Mayu asked anxiously, clutching the bed-sheets around her knees.

"I'm going to see a friend who owns a little organic farm just outside of town. We're going to take some acid." Robert left without finishing his coffee. After the bang of the closing door,

Mayu heard his footsteps recede in the hallway, and then stillness prevailed.

In love? I'm in love with him, she thought. How did that happen? There's no way I can drive him from my mind. He's out there taking LSD and I'm worried sick about him. What's happening with him? It reminds me of my father on a binge. But then, maybe it's not the same thing. LSD is not alcohol, and Robert is not my father.

Could David be wrong about Cynthia? Could he be trying to create a gulf between Robert and me for his own purposes?

But then, why has Robert started having sexual problems with me all of a sudden? Is there a connection between his seeing Cynthia and his having difficulty with me?

Yet, if he wants me to lose weight, then it means he *does* care and he *is* serious about me. If losing a few pounds will solve the problem, then I should go ahead and do it. True, I have put on some weight. When I went to the Student Health Center for the pregnancy test, I weighed 175 pounds. So I guess I'll see if I can get some help with a diet.

But at the same time, didn't Dorothy Parker get it exactly right when she wrote:

> *They hail you as their morning star*
> *Because you are the way you are.*
> *If you return the sentiment*
> *They want to make you different.*

I don't know. It's all so confusing! Mayu could not sleep and she could not read. Her mind raced all through the night, her thoughts turning over and over. Still, she didn't know what to think.

Weeks went by. Mayu didn't hear from Robert. She heard about him, though. He had a birthday party; she was not invited. She heard from different people, David included, that Cynthia had been there. As the winter semester progressed, Mayu found it hard to concentrate on anything that she was supposed to be doing.

One mid-December afternoon, while hopelessly trying to study for finals, she heard the sound of steps. When she looked up, there he was, standing before her, as if she had conjured him with her thoughts. "Hello," she greeted him, trying to keep her tone normal. Her voice threatened to choke and tears welled up.

"It's been a while since I've seen you, and it will be a while before I see you again. I'm going home for Christmas."

"Where have you been? You haven't been to any of the classes we have together."

"I'm taking incompletes in them. I'll pick things up again after New Year's."

There were a dozen hurtful, indignant and sarcastic things sitting on the tip of Mayu's tongue; words that would have jolted him out of his casual insouciance. But she suppressed herself and chose only to say, "Have a good Christmas."

"What are your plans?" Robert asked.

"I was thinking of going to Oregon and spending the Christmas holidays with Betsy Vogelsang. She and I have been friends from the time I was working as a camp counselor out there."

"You have a good Christmas, too," Robert said. He sauntered over and kissed her on the top of her head. Then he walked out of the library.

Mayu thought, I know that there's chemistry between Robert and me. What could be greater evidence than the charge I just felt when he talked to me? But why does he treat me like this? How does he really feel about me? Things are so confused.

Mayu did fly to Portland. When she landed, Oregon seemed a totally different world from the frozen Minnesota that she had left behind. Betsy had been married and divorced since Mayu had last seen her, and now she lived alone in a two-bedroom apartment on the outskirts of town. She was happy to have company on the first Christmas since her divorce. The two women tried to find refuge and comfort in each other. They put up a Christmas tree, as well as a brave front. They also cooked a festive dinner and exchanged gifts. But then something happened—both women's courage failed at the same time. Each was so consumed with desolation that neither had the strength to comfort the other.

While Betsy had crying jags, Mayu had diarrhea. Though she had initially planned to stay through New Year's, Mayu decided to return to Minneapolis just after Christmas.

When she arrived on campus, to her surprise, she found Robert there. He was surprised to see how much weight she had lost and expressed his admiration through an honest desire for her.

One afternoon, they drove to Minnehaha Falls, beautifully frozen in ice cascades at that time of year. They ate the sandwiches Mayu had brought and talked about where their relationship now stood. Mayu had missed him so acutely when she was in Oregon that she had literally made herself sick. She was too proud to admit it, though, and didn't utter a word to him about her experience there. The specter of Cynthia still loomed large, but it was a subject she wanted Robert to broach.

"Mayu, you're everything I want a woman to be. Now, even your figure is beginning to meet my specifications."

"I'm so glad I meet your approval," Mayu responded, with an edge of irony in her voice.

"I did a lot of thinking about us over the Christmas holidays," Robert said, totally missing her sarcasm. "Anyway, I came to the conclusion that I can't live without you."

As if a dam had burst inside her, Mayu began to wail. Finally, she thought, Robert has chosen me over Cynthia. That night, Robert and Mayu met again at the Summers's house for dinner. Afterwards, while the other graduate students socialized with their professor and his wife, Mayu and Robert stole out of the house and went for a walk. Hand in hand, they strolled through the ice-covered landscape. Robert stopped, took Mayu in his arms and said, "Although I have come to love you, I will always remain a wanderer."

Mayu heard his words, but in this moment of closeness she didn't heed what he was saying. Their lips united and they stayed entwined, warm in each other's arms, in the frozen night. As they walked back to join the group, Robert and Mayu decided to move in together right away.

They spent the night together at his apartment. A noise woke Mayu. She looked at the clock—it was 6:00 a.m. Robert was sitting in front of the mirror with a nylon stocking on his head.

"What are you doing?" she asked in a hoarse voice.

Without looking around at her, he said, "I'm straightening my hair."

"Oh. All right," she said, doubtfully. She went back to sleep, dreaming that Robert was on his way to tell Cynthia that it was all over between them.

****

The mounds of shoveled snow that had piled up on sidewalks, lawns and parking lots had disappeared. Greenery was gradually unfolding all over the campus. The onset of spring was evident in the eyes of young lovers. Mayu and Robert had been living together all winter. At Mayu's urging, and with her assistance, Robert had cleared his incompletes. He was looking into the possibility of a scholarship to write a dissertation on hippies. Mayu's experience and research on young people for Finnish broadcasting would come in handy. He may have been living a liberated 60's life, but he couldn't shake off his conventional upbringing. He started to talk of marriage.

With each passing day, Mayu's Fulbright was getting closer to the end. They paid a visit to the office of the Immigration and Naturalization Service and were told that Mayu had only until July to stay in the United States. Then she had to go back to Finland for at least two years to fulfill the Fulbright requirements. But if they got married, then the two-year requirement would be waived. Marriage seemed the inevitable choice.

In May of 1970, the couple and some university friends gathered at a farm near New Prague, Minnesota. A judge drove up in an old Thunderbird to marry them. Both bride and groom wore blue jeans and beads. Mayu promised to love, but not necessarily to obey, then the couple and their guests ate a dinner of food grilled over an open fire. Robert took out an LSD tab and shared it with Mayu. They separated from the group and went into the woods. There were wildflowers growing everywhere. Mayu and Robert took off their clothes to lie down in the flowers. Dizzily, vividly, they made love. Mayu thought that the sky and the trees and the flowers choreographed a whirling, rhythmic dance timed perfectly to the movements of their love-making. She was giddy with the lustiness of her experience, every nerve vibrating with an explosion of colors. She thought, Everything in the entire universe is benevolent and lovely. Mayu had never known this feeling before.

When they returned and rejoined their wedding guests, Mayu's expansive feelings had disappeared. Suddenly, she couldn't stand the people there anymore. She felt that she could see their thoughts hovering over their heads like cartoon captions, revealing their unsavory motives and lurid secret dreams.

When night fell, Robert and Mayu spread their sleeping bag by the pond beneath the starry sky. They made love again, then, entirely exhausted, they went to sleep. The LSD gave Mayu vivid, highly colored dreams all night long. When she awoke, she found that she couldn't remember details—only a general feeling of having been surrounded by extraordinary beauty. She heard Robert say, "I've been up for quite a while, but I didn't want to wake you. You were sleeping so peacefully and looked so beautiful." He took Mayu in his arms and she felt completely safe. Farther down along the curves of the pond, other lovers still slept. Mayu and Robert crawled out of the sleeping bag, pulled on their clothes and slipped away before the others awoke.

CHAPTER SIX

1960

When 14-year old Mayu arrived at the confirmation camp, she felt very certain about how she felt toward God, Man, and religion. Despite her mother's insistence that she go, she was less sure of the experience that she was going to have at camp. Time and time again, her father had told her that there was no scientific evidence to support belief in the existence of God, and lots of evidence to cast doubt on it. After all, he told Mayu, "How likely is it that a fatherly Being woke up one morning and created the universe? It's more plausible that our earth was formed from planetary dust, and that life on earth arose from scientific accident and mutation, not some divine blueprint. These are things for which there is real evidence, not just superstitious belief." He added, "Religions not only make fools of believers, but herd them into churches and impose illegitimate authority and control over them. Religion reinforces social inequality and injustice."

These were big ideas for the mind of a young girl, but her father had repeated them to her so often that they had become a part of her thinking. But at this old farmhouse, away from the materialism and pretension of urban life, Mayu was willing to engage in a discussion about God and religion. Fourteen other girls her age, her fellow campers, dumped their bags on the bunks that they were provided and immediately agreed that they would get closer to God by immersing themselves in Nature. Mayu offered no argument. All Finns, it seemed, were children of Nature, and Mayu felt this with a special passion. They all hiked up a trail in the neighboring hills, feeling the unusually warm summer sun and relishing the berries they found. Mayu shrieked with joy when they found a patch of chanterelle mushrooms. She picked several, wrapped them in her handkerchief and placed the little bundle in her shirt pocket. Later, in the evening, the girls sat in the sauna until the heat opened their pores and sweat poured from their bodies.

By the time they sat under the starry sky around a blazing fire, they were mellow and receptive. As they began their discussion, the girls cooked sausages on the fire. Always quick to take intellectual stands, Mayu now felt swept up by the mood of the moment. Here in this beautiful pastoral setting, with the sparks from the fire rising and dissolving into the darkness, she looked around at the girls' faces aglow with fervor, and felt in her heart that she was in communion with a super-Being. She spent two weeks at the camp and came away a believer.

Once back home, she put on a white jacket, white skirt and white shoes, spread a thin coat of beige make-up over her pale skin, and arrived at the church with her mother to find it full of parents, friends and relatives. To her surprise, her father was there, with Lasse. Both looked drunk. The minister began the catechism, a sort of spiritual examination, and Mayu received the most difficult question: "Why do we believe in God?"

"It's not so much by logic or scientific evidence but by faith that we believe in God," she answered in a very strong and convincing voice. As she spoke, she could hear her father muttering something. Then, he burped and giggled. Mayu was sure that everybody had heard him and felt embarrassed, but tried not to let it interfere with what she was doing. She went up to the altar to receive her first communion. As she swallowed the bread and drank the wine, she felt one with Christ. The fervor this stirred within her was powerful. Her religion teacher at school later expressed amazement at the transformation of her attitude.

Not long after her confirmation, Mayu pulled the one good dress she had out of the closet and went to her very first formal dance. The boys were lined up against the wall on one side of the room in the community center. The girls were on the other side, studiously preening, crossing and uncrossing their legs. Some hiked their skirts up their thighs before stealing looks at the boys to see if they were being noticed. Mayu hated this grotesque charade. She felt like a cut of beef in a butcher shop. Still, she decided to stay. "When in Rome, do as the Romans do," she sighed to herself. She even accepted a dance with a boy. As the tempo of the music increased, she began to dance vigorously. Every thought flew out of her head—a rare moment in Mayu's life—and she felt pure animal pleasure in the swaying of her body and her rapidly beating heart.

All of a sudden, she felt something slip under her dress. Before she could do anything about it, the "thing" landed on the floor. The boy stepped on the cup-shaped, rubber object. He looked at it in confusion, then his eyes opened wide. He exclaimed, "Your bra pad fell out!" His words were heard by many couples dancing nearby. One or two of the young people stared at Mayu and grinned. She picked up the hated object and stormed off the dance floor to a ripple of laughter.

In the building's lobby, an older woman who had seen what had happened put her arm around the girl and said, "My dear, worse things than this have happened here. You're standing at this very moment over a pit where thousands of Reds were buried after they were shot. It's hard to believe, but the city erected this building right over their mass grave."

Mayu was stunned. The pain of her humiliation on the dance floor suddenly seemed trivial in comparison. She thanked the woman. But she had no desire to return to the dance, so she left the building. She walked home slowly, her head bent; in her mind's eye, she could see thousands of soldiers lying in the pit, blood oozing from their wounds, as they screamed in agony until they died. And here she was, worried about losing a silly bra pad. Her selfishness put her to shame.

One day, Mayu was sitting at the kitchen table when she noticed a prominent article on the front page of the newspaper, *Lahden Sanomat*. Toini Kajander, an influential man about town, had died on the steps of the bus terminal. He was very fat; heart failure was diagnosed as the cause of death. When she finished the article, she turned the page in search of other news. Tucked away on the tenth page, in small type, was a brief report about thousands of people dying of starvation in India.

Mayu laid the newspaper down on her knees and looked thoughtfully out the window. Was the life of one white man who ate himself into the grave more valuable than the lives of so many thousands of brown people? What is wrong with the world's values? she wondered.

Mayu visited her father every Friday afternoon. One day, her mother accompanied her. When they arrived at his house, they found him lying on the floor in a drunken stupor, bottles scattered all around him. The air was permeated with a foul odor. It wasn't long before they found the source of the stench. Her mother took off Aarne's fouled pants, wiped him clean and managed to pull some fresh pants on him. Then, she heated the soup she had brought from the bank kitchen and sat down to feed him. Mayu couldn't believe what she was seeing. Her mother had been mistreated, beaten and then deserted by her father. Yet, here she was, cleaning and caring for him. If Mayu visited him and cared for him, she had no choice. He's my only father and we are connected by an irreplaceable bond, she said to herself. But my mother has no such natural bond with him. She could divorce Aarne and remarry. As a matter of fact, Mayu would have loved to see her mother with another man who could bring some happiness into her barren life. While Mayu admired Raija for her dedication as a mother, she could never understand her behavior toward her father.

Mayu was enraged when she discovered that the inheritance her father had spoken of, the one that he and Lasse were spending on liquor and women, had amounted to 40,000 Marks. This equated to 21 years of her mother's salary—while she and her mother didn't have the money to buy milk and bread. It was clear to Mayu that alcoholism was Finland's worst social problem. She would get very upset when she saw drunken men on the streets, staggering, panhandling and being a nuisance. To her, the bottle seemed a devil—out to destroy marriages, families and eventually, the whole of society.

Another dance was scheduled—this time at her school. Mayu loved dancing and she was determined not to let her previous horrible experience deter her from going. Her peers, especially the girls, were all excited about the upcoming event. When the big day finally arrived, the greatest concern of her female classmates was, "What am I going to wear?" Mayu heard those words again and again during class breaks and at lunchtime. When she couldn't take it any more, she burst out, "Why don't you do what I'm planning to do...go naked!" Her sarcasm cast a pall over the giggling girls. But it also put a stop to their endless silly discussions about their clothes—at least in Mayu's presence.

Mayu left school for home. She walked slowly and talked earnestly to herself, as was her habit, about the afternoon's experience. Can there be two realities, one for the girls and one for me? she wondered. Head down, she walked along, occasionally bumping into passers-by, letting her feet find their own way home. But, she decided, in the final analysis, there can be only one reality. Obviously, in the present case, it cannot be theirs, she argued to herself. Not only because, in spite of the innumerable clothes they possess, they seem to see a problem, but because clothing, or any other possession for that matter, is a state of mind, an attitude, a personal ideology. To them, having many clothes is more complicated than having none. I don't have any clothes and I don't have any problems, so I must be closer to reality. If I'm closer to reality in this regard and if I feel the same way about other material things, then I must be having a true and real existence.

That night, she walked out onto the dance floor wearing the dress and shoes that she had worn a thousand times before. The dancing had already begun and bodies draped in beautiful dresses were shaking all over the floor. Mayu smiled and thought to herself, was all that anxiety for this trivial moment?

"Would you like to dance?" The words startled her. She turned around and saw a smiling boy. She nodded and they began to dance. Soon, she discovered that they danced well together. She liked the way the boy looked. He was tall, thin and blond, with an aquiline nose and a broad forehead. Someone dimmed the lights and the tempo of the music slowed. The bodies of the young couples came closer and closer together, where they began to gently sway in place. The boy held Mayu close and wrapped his arms tighter and tighter until she felt something hard in his pants pocket.

A liquor bottle, she thought in disgust and struggled to loosen herself from his grip. She caught a brief glimpse of the boy's stunned face before she tore away from him and dashed out of the hall.

All weekend, Mayu brooded that all men were nothing but drunks. When she returned to school on Monday, the boy accosted her during recess. "What happened at the dance? What did I do to you?"

"My father is an alcoholic, so I get very upset with people who drink. During the dance, I felt a liquor bottle in your pants pocket and it upset me very much."

The boy laughed and his face reddened to the roots of his hair. "I'm embarrassed to say that it was not a bottle…definitely not a liquor bottle."

"Well," she said stiffly, "I hope you're telling me the truth."

"Cross my heart. By the way, my name's Saku Kajala."

"I'm Mayu Kaariainen."

"I'm very happy to make a formal acquaintance with you. Now that the misunderstanding has been removed, perhaps we can be friends?"

They began to spend time together, taking walks and talking for hours.

****

One day, Mayu went to see her mother at the bank and found her receiving instructions from the bank director. In walked her friend Saku.

"What are you doing here?" Mayu could not resist the question.

"I'm here to see the bank director," he answered.

"Do you have business with him? Are you planning to work in the bank?"

"Neither. He's my father."

Mayu was flabbergasted.

"What brings you here?" Saku countered.

Mayu paused for a moment and then pointed to Raija. "My mother works here. I've come to see her."

"That cleaning woman is your mother?"

"Yes." Mayu could see the sudden confusion on Saku's face, along with his contempt for her class. It was unbearable. She loved the boy, but she couldn't stand to see her mother being humiliated in his eyes. When Mayu left the bank, she realized the monumental difference in their social stations and didn't think they would ever be together again. But whether or not she could be with Saku, she was determined not to feel embarrassed about her humble background. For one thing, she said to herself, she wasn't responsible for her life condition, only for what she made of herself, as Anna Macki had told her years ago. But she had come to feel love for Saku and now this materialistic, misguided world was taking him away from her.

Back in school during the lunch hour, she sat alone at a corner table and tried to come to grips with her feelings. She heard footsteps and sensed someone approaching her. It was Saku. "May I sit down?" he asked.

"I guess so."

Saku pulled up a chair. "I've been getting a hard time from my parents. They want me to stop seeing you. My mother can't stand the idea that her son is in love with the daughter of a cleaning woman. But I don't want to stop seeing you. Could we meet secretly?"

"I guess so," Mayu answered. She was uncharacteristically quiet, as she struggled to make sense of her feelings. Saku quickly got up and was gone.

They met secretly, sometimes at the house of her best friend, Aini, and sometimes in the city park under the cover of night. After a while, though, the degradation of being a "back-door woman" began to grate on her nerves. She was a person with a passion for openness, equality and acceptance.

"If you want me, Saku," Mayu finally told him one night when they were in the park, "you will either have to see me in view of the whole world, or try to forget me."

"I couldn't do that," Saku responded.

At first, Mayu hoped he meant that he couldn't forget her. But it soon became clear that he was not willing to defy his parents and see her openly.

"I don't believe in this kind of hypocrisy," Mayu mumbled to herself. "If I am not good enough to be seen with him in public, then he is not good enough to for me, either. I'll kill my memory of him."

"What are you mumbling, Mayu?" her mother asked, raising her head from her knitting.

"I have decided not to love Saku anymore."

****

As he did every year, Mr. Toivonranta, Mayu's principal as well as her history teacher, invited the graduating class to his house. His wife served them a hearty meal, which relaxed everyone. They settled down to play a game of *Truth or Dare*. Someone asked a question and then a bottle was spun on the floor. Whomever the bottle pointed to was supposed to answer the question, and come up with the next query. The bottle was spun several times and the guests laughed uproariously at the answers. Finally, the bottle was spun and came to a stop, pointing toward Mayu. Her question was, "What is the ultimate goal of life?"

Mayu's face took on the serious expression that was so familiar to the people who knew her. "My ultimate goal," she said, "is to find a cause worth dying for. I want to have a calling, like Joan of Arc. Until I find that calling, I want to be engaged in a search for the meaning of life. Why am I here? What should I do with my life? What is my place in society? Should my duty be limited to my country or should it transcend national or racial lines?" Mayu emphasized that she was still grappling with the issues and had none of the answers, but she felt strongly that an individual's existence should make the quality of life on this earth better. "There is no reason why poverty, hunger, discrimination and human exploitation should continue.

"We haven't even been taught about our own civil war, in which a lot of blood was shed in an ideological struggle," she said, eyeing Mr. Toivonranta reprovingly. "The rivalry between the Soviet Union and the United States," she said, "by promoting guns, is depriving people all over the world of butter. The quality of life on this planet would dramatically improve, if the weapons industry were to close down tomorrow. Otherwise," she concluded, "we stand on the brink of annihilation."

Mayu's monologue brought the game to a grinding halt. The mood of gaiety was replaced by a somber atmosphere. Mr. Toivonranta said, "Mayu, you remember the day I came looking for you and found you playing in the little tunnel? Today, I feel that it was a great day for the both of us. I feel a great sense of pride in you."

Never one at a loss for words, Mayu opened her mouth to say something else when the group was interrupted by the abrupt entry of a teenager they had never seen before. He was a huge, hulking boy with a curiously blank face. He lumbered into the center of the circle of students and, making an undecipherable sound, grabbed the game bottle. Mayu realized that this boy must Mr. Toivonranta's son and that he was severely mentally retarded. The teacher blushed and stammered out an apology, looking very ashamed.

Mayu's heart flamed with outrage. How shallow our principal is, to feel ashamed of this boy. Is the boy responsible for being mentally retarded? He can't help being slow any more than I can help being poor, she thought. We were both born with our disadvantages and it disgusts me that his father feels shame about it. As her feelings of identification with the boy grew, she felt the eight years she had respected the principal fade to nothing. She immediately judged that he was unworthy of her admiration. She felt relieved that her education at his school was coming to an end. Now, she would never have to see him again.

CHAPTER SEVEN

1970

The first ray of daylight filtered softly through the lace curtains of Robert's boyhood bedroom. Locked in each other's arms, Robert and Mayu were still sound asleep. Since they had not told either of their families that they were already married, they had been provided separate rooms. At some point the previous night, they had decided to go to bed together anyway. Suddenly, the door burst open, and before they had a chance to focus their eyes and take stock of the situation, Robert felt the thump of a fist on his forehead. Mayu's eyes opened on a beefy hand, shaking Robert awake. As she looked up, she saw Robert's father's stern face and imposing figure.

"Robert, we want to see you in the living room." Mayu got up and slipped into the bathroom, closing the door behind her. If Robert was going to get a dressing down from his parents, she didn't want to be present. Late the previous evening, after the long drive from Minnesota, Mayu and Robert had arrived in Cayahoga Falls, Ohio. She had not anticipated waking up the next day in quite this fashion. When she finally came out of the bathroom, Robert was still with his parents. The three of them gave off the self-conscious gloom of participants at a wake. Mayu's polite "good morning" was met with a stern salvo from Robert's mother:

"You wouldn't do this in your mother's house."

"Oh yes, I would. I have!" Mayu fired back, without realizing the implications until it was too late. The rest of their stay was marked by a distinct chill from Robert's parents. As the two young people prepared to leave for Finland, Robert's parents made their pronouncement. "We won't be attending the wedding," they said.

If Robert was upset, he didn't let on to Mayu, and he assumed an air of nonchalance. Mayu felt very odd about his parents' behavior, but kept her thoughts to herself. She realized that her spontaneity had already caused enough damage.

****

Mayu's brother, Heikki, and his lovely wife, Sinikka, with whom Mayu had become very close since Heikki and she were married, welcomed Mayu and Robert to Finland as future bride and groom. They didn't have any relatives in Lahti, except for Mayu's mother. Her father had been dead for six years now, but there were many acquaintances and friends from Mayu's school days. Invitations were hastily issued and preparations speedily made. Shortly after landing in Helsinki, Mayu had gone shopping and bought a pair of red and white trousers, along with a white blouse, from a little shop at the waterfront. She put them on in preparation for the wedding. Robert dressed in a cream-colored suit and decided not to wear a tie.

When they arrived at the church in Heikki's car, their friends were already gathered there. A few minutes later, Raija, escorted by Eino, arrived in a taxi. As arranged, the organist began to play Simon and Garfunkel's *Sounds of Silence*, and the ceremony began. The couple exchanged rings and promised to stay together until death did them part. It seemed to Mayu that the ceremony was over in a flash. It was as short as they had wanted. Now, they were properly wedded by a Lutheran minister. The bride, who didn't look very bride-like, was kissed by all the men in attendance. When it was Eino's turn, rather than simply kissing her, he clung around her neck, wept bitterly and would not let go. Heikki had to forcibly pry him loose. Eino stumbled out of the church, broken-hearted. The entire scene put a damper on the festive occasion. Before Robert understood what had just taken place, Heikki pulled him aside and said, "Be good to my sister, or else..."

They all went to Heikki's house for a wedding reception. It was a simple affair consisting of coffee, pastries and strawberries. Raija, Heikki and Sinikka all wanted to talk to Robert, but none of them spoke English. Mayu translated for them.

"He's a great catch!" Mayu's sister-in-law whispered to her. They all seemed to be overwhelmed by this tall, handsome young American who had deigned to marry into the family. What impressed Mayu's mother was that although he was upper-class, he was so humble and down-to-earth. She felt as if all of her prayers for Mayu's happiness had been answered.

Now that the church wedding was over, it was time for them to get on with the business of life, work and building a future together. Robert chose Copenhagen as the venue for the preparation of his doctoral comprehensive exams and the collection of data for his dissertation. Mayu's visa situation required that she stay out of the United States for a while. Both felt pleased with the choice of Denmark.

When the couple arrived in Copenhagen, they settled into an apartment downtown. While Robert buckled down to a schedule of 12-hour-a-day study for his comps, Mayu took a job at a candy factory. She amused herself during her leisure hours by strolling in the notorious red light district. It was a fairly settled and mundane life, punctuated by the antics of their flamboyant Moroccan neighbor, who complained bitterly about the scarcity of couscous and dates in Denmark. Now and again, the couple would drift off into the mellow and dream-like world of hashish and marijuana.

Robert arranged to take his comprehensive exams by mail. The questions arrived from the University of Minnesota in a sealed envelope. When he sat down to tackle them, he did not stop writing until he was finished in the early hours of the following morning. When he was done, they both felt a great sense of relief.

That night, they put on a Beatles record, rolled three marijuana cigarettes and snuggled together on the couch to experience what their heightened senses could absorb. Mayu was surprised at how distinct each instrument on the record became. When a horn was playing, she felt she was sitting inside a horn and could put out her hand and feel the smooth metal on each side. The vibrations seemed to mix with the pulsing of her blood. Mayu and Robert made love and she felt that beating blood roar until it burst into flowers and fireworks.

It was August. When Mayu's period didn't come, she went to see a doctor, who confirmed that she was pregnant. She took a train to Stockholm and, from there, boarded a boat to Finland to see her mother. Instead of being delighted, Raija was troubled. "What kind of way is this to bring a child into the world?" her mother asked. "You're going to be here and your husband is going to return to America?" It was true; Robert had to be back for the spring term and Mayu couldn't get a visa to go back to the United States yet.

Mayu made a quick, cold decision that she would not have this baby after all, if Robert could not be with her. The next afternoon, she went to Helsinki for an abortion.

Mayu had always been proud of her mind and her decisive character. When she underwent this abortion and made a rapid physical recovery, she thought, *That's that.* But in years to come, the life that she had lost haunted her in subtle ways; ways that she didn't anticipate at the time.

Before the year had rung out, Mayu was pregnant again. This time, the couple opted to try harder to get a visa for her. They traveled to Helsinki and persuaded the consul at the American Embassy to give Mayu a visa for travel to the United States. It was for only six months—"but it's a start," they told each other.

Mayu bid farewell once again to her beloved mother and her equally beloved Finland. They traveled to Luxembourg to take a cheap flight to New York.

At the Luxembourg Airport, they had several hours to kill. They met Sandy and Joe, two young men bound for Ohio, and struck up an acquaintance. All four settled down in the passenger concourse. Sandy pulled out a faded deck of cards and they played Hearts. During the game, Sandy and Joe confided to Mayu and Robert that they were carrying hashish which they were planning to smuggle into the United States.

"You'll never make it through Customs looking that way," Mayu warned. The two did look as though they had just walked off the set of *Easy Rider.*

"You'll see," Sandy responded, nonchalantly. He lit a hashish pipe and offered Mayu and Robert a toke. Robert looked around in consternation. What if we're spotted by the airport police? But no police appeared and the four young people safely boarded the plane and slept soundly all the way across the Atlantic.

When the plane was an hour or so away from landing at JFK Airport, Sandy casually got up, stretched and, bag in hand, disappeared into the bathroom. When he returned to his seat, he had gone through such a transformation that Mayu didn't immediately recognize him. He was clean-shaven, bespectacled and was wearing a blue suit. Still, the people at Customs gave him a thorough going-over, while he nonchalantly stood, smoking a cigarette and winking at Mayu. When the examination was over and the Customs officials couldn't find anything damaging on him, Sandy exited the terminal, bursting with jubilation.

"I did it! I did it!" he shouted and took the wad of hashish out of his mouth and displayed it proudly. He had the world's shortest career as a young executive. Within minutes, he reverted to blue jeans, sweatshirt and cowboy boots.

The two men had left behind a Karmann Ghia two-seater in New York. When they picked it up, they offered Mayu and Robert a ride as far as Ohio. It was quite a memorable experience for three men and a pregnant woman to cram into the tiny sports car and drive all the way to Ohio in a swirling snowstorm. From Ohio, Mayu and Robert took the Greyhound bus to Minnesota.

As the spring term and Mayu's pregnancy progressed, they settled into an apartment complex on campus. Mayu was not used to the idea of being just a housewife, so she got involved in the literature search for Robert's dissertation. When the results were announced and Robert had passed the comps, they celebrated again. This time, the celebration was of a different kind. Mayu was almost three months into her pregnancy and they didn't smoke pot or make passionate love. They had a few friends over and served a buffet dinner.

"I'm so happy," Mayu finally admitted to herself. She paused and considered her words. Never before had she said this. Even now, she acknowledged this emotion grudgingly, as though it were a subversive force sapping her strength.

She looked forward to going to dinner with her friends Jim and Susan the following evening. Jim had also passed his comps and Susan had decided to prepare a quiet dinner for four at their apartment. Susan had a reputation as a beauty, but wasn't much of a cook. The dinner she served was adequate, but Mayu smugly thought that Susan couldn't touch her in the culinary department. Mayu didn't eat very much, although she did join in the conversation. She felt too indolent to help with the cleanup. Robert, however, jumped up from his seat to help Susan. They made several trips to the kitchen and each time, they took longer to return. Mayu and Jim were in the living room, discussing Scandinavian social welfare policy. When Susan and Robert had been gone a long time and all was quiet in the kitchen, Mayu got up to get a glass of water—only to discover Susan and Robert kissing passionately by the sink.

Mayu's stomach heaved with nausea. She did not feel like challenging them, or even speaking. She went to the bathroom and vehemently vomited Susan's food into the toilet bowl. Mayu and Robert left the house abruptly, using Mayu's pregnancy and her supposedly delicate state as a pretext. On their way to the apartment, Mayu tried to find words for her agony.

In his characteristic way, Robert merely dismissed her emotion as the ravings of a hysterical woman. "Nothing happened!" he insisted, with a broad gesture of his hand over the steering wheel. "You're imagining things."

He parked the car. Mayu knew she hadn't hallucinated. She felt betrayed. Once again, her happy world was shattered. She was determined, though, not to let Robert know how she felt. I'll do my suffering in silence, she vowed.

A few days later, Robert responded to an advertisement; Harvard was looking for a sociologist to move down to Bogota, Colombia to work on a project funded by the National Institute of Child Health and Development. He was called for an interview in Cambridge and was selected on the spot. He was asked to take up his post immediately.

After Robert left, Mayu had a few weeks alone to comfort herself. She re-established contact with her former advisor, Jerry Summers, who made her feel better. Her former classmate, David Howard, also dropped by often. She could converse with him for hours on any subject. She liked to talk to him about a notion she had to create a sort of expanded public library, where not only books but clothing, furniture, tools, and other things could be borrowed for free. These discussions kept her amused and occupied.

Mayu was married, she was pregnant and she loved Robert, so she didn't have any choice but to keep going. True, Robert had hurt her, but he had also once warned her about his nature—"I'll always remain a wanderer." So what happened should not come as a surprise, she thought. Though the thought crossed her mind, she could not really fight back using another man as a weapon—*at least while I'm pregnant.*

****

It was May and the smell of lilac filled the air. Almost overnight, the earth was covered with a carpet of moist green grass, while tiny buds peeked out from the branches after waking from a long, harsh winter. Mayu drank in the changing season; Minnesota looked so much like her beloved Finland. She loved the clear air and the sense that there was always a forest nearby. She hated to leave this land and the friends that she had made in the previous year. But she had also been hurt here. It will be best, she decided, if I leave that hurt behind me if I can. She prepared to join Robert in Colombia.

When she arrived at the Minneapolis Airport, she was surprised to find a large group of friends and acquaintances who had come to say good-bye. Before she had a chance to catch her breath and take everything in, there was a tap on her shoulder. She turned around and found Susan standing there, looking sheepish. She took Mayu's hands in hers and said, almost in a whisper, "I want to apologize. Robert is so sensuous that I couldn't help myself."

"Sure you could have," Mayu wanted to say. But she bit her lip, smiled and brushed the tension aside. "It's all in the past now," she said, giving Susan a reassuring touch.

Jerry Summers walked up to her and put his arm around her. "I'm going to miss you," he said. "Who's going to have such dramatic emotional crises now that you're going?"

Mayu smiled. "We've shared some very delicate moments," she said and gave him a kiss on the cheek, knowing full well that he wanted it on the lips. David Howard came forward and hugged her, making sure that he did not press her seven-months-pregnant belly. When they parted after a long hug, she was too choked up to utter a word. She finally found her voice and said good-bye to all of her friends. She was embarking on a new phase of life, thinking she would never be returning again. She boarded the jet. Once it was airborne, she said to herself, "How much effort it takes to turn the last page of a chapter!"

****

Mayu joined Robert in the duplex that he had rented in Bogota. Her first order of business was to find an obstetrician. She was delighted with the one she found, Dr. Mondragon, whom she quickly grew to trust. A few weeks later, Mayu went into labor. It was a protracted birthing, but the presence of Robert and her doctor soothed her.

"It's a boy," the doctor said. The sound of her son's first cries was the sweetest she had ever heard. Mayu had always seen motherhood as one of her life's goals and having a child gave her special joy. Friends, neighbors and colleagues came in droves to congratulate Robert and Mayu on the birth of their first baby. Women adored the downy blond hair rising from his shapely little head, his button-like blue eyes peeking out at the new world and his miniature hands, trying to discover their usefulness.

He was an unusually contented baby and almost never cried. He would grunt when he was hungry or wet, just to let Mayu know his problem. A friend of Mayu's, a harried mother herself, remarked, "How peaceful your baby is! I have never seen one who would sleep 7:00 a.m. to 7:00 p.m. without waking his mother." Mayu named him Hannu and Robert didn't seem to object to this very Finnish name.

There was one thing that tarnished Mayu's joy in Hannu. The other half of their duplex was occupied by a Colombian man and his American wife who were in mourning over the recent death of their newborn. It was hard to enjoy Hannu with a bereaved mother on the other side of their wall. Mayu wished she could have comforted the other woman, but her own gain where the other had lost made it too awkward.

Despite her passion for openness, Mayu felt that she needed privacy so she could freely enjoy her happiness. She yearned for a bigger house with a garden, so that they wouldn't have to feel like "rats in a cage," as she put it. Robert's American income gave them so much buying power in Colombia that they could shop for a house and live well on a single paycheck.

The moment she saw the house, Mayu loved it. It had a cathedral ceiling with beams covered in a deep maroon cloth. The loft had two bedrooms and a den. The house was not big and didn't have much more space than the duplex, but its design and wooden structure appealed to Mayu's aesthetic sense. She liked its seclusion, surrounded as it was by almost half an acre of land. . She and Robert made the decision to buy it overnight and moved into it within a week. The move turned out to be a great relief. With a brand new baby and a new home in a new country, Mayu hoped that the unpleasant episodes of the past would be behind them now and that Robert would change for the better.

Since childhood, Mayu had always had a negative attitude about having servants. She had always believed that hiring domestics was tantamount to owning slaves. She was determined that she would never be party to such exploitation. But after she settled down in her new house and began to know Bogota and its people, her opinion changed. She realized that there were many poor and unskilled people in Colombia who would welcome a chance to work as domestics. Because she had a new baby, Mayu also found that she did need a helping hand, so she hired Maria, a 17 year-old girl.

With a servant at home to cook and look after Hannu, Mayu took a job as a psychologist with Robert's Harvard project. Within a year, she became the chief psychologist on the project. It was hard work, so she drank a lot more caffeine than she ever had before. Still, she thrived on the challenge and the pressure. The project was concerned with how nutrition and environment affected prenatal development. The subjects of the study were Colombia's poor. Having been poor herself, Mayu felt strong empathy with them. Also, now that she had a child of her own, she felt a special bond with struggling mothers, as well as a responsibility toward them. Her conscientious work and innate ability fueled her rapid promotion.

Her office was down the hall from Robert's and they found their working relationship exceptionally congenial. Each found it easy to understand the other's communication, picking up meaning from just a few words, or a gesture—a raised eyebrow or a shrug. People were amazed to see how well they seemed to blend their professional and personal lives. Unfortunately, though, other project staffers didn't find Mayu easy to work with. They found her abrasive, opinionated, inflexible and sometimes outright obnoxious. The news of her promotion had to be withheld from the Colombian staffers for fear that discontent would burst into open resentment.

Mayu was always looking for Scandinavians, especially Finns, and whenever she would see them in stores, theaters, restaurants, or on the street, she would approach them, strike up a conversation and invite them to her house. One of the people she met was Paivi, a young woman from Helsinki married to a Colombian man named Edgar Gomez. She was not very bright or educated, but she was Finnish just the same.

Shortly after she started visiting Mayu, she became the focus of Robert's attention. Once, when Mayu saw Robert playing footsie with her under the table, she said to him, "Robert, would you please lay off? If you don't care about me, at least look out for yourself. Her husband strikes me as the jealous sort."

"I don't know what you're talking about," Robert said in an accusatory tone, as if the whole thing were a figment of Mayu's paranoid imagination. Meanwhile, he went on doing just what he had been doing under the table.

As Mayu was preparing for her annual summer visit to Finland, Paivi came to see her and offered to look after her dog, Mishka, a female collie. "That would be very helpful," Mayu said, and took her up on her offer. Paivi had a simpering way of looking at Mayu, designed to hide her embarrassment at being the object of Robert's attentions. It was a look that Mayu chose to ignore.

A few days later, Paivi's husband, Edgar, came to see Mayu and asked if she would be willing to bring some clothes back from

Finland for their young son. "Of course, no problem," Mayu responded in her usual animated style. He then produced a sealed envelope from his jacket pocket. Holding it tentatively in her hand, she asked, "What's this? You don't need to pay me now."

"No, no. These are clothes measurements."

Some premonition told Mayu that there was more to his gesture than the mere giving of measurements. But she chose not to say anything and stuck the envelope in her pocketbook.

When Robert, Mayu and Hannu arrived in Helsinki, Mayu took off just one day to recover from jet lag before heading down to Stockmann's Department store. She got some clothes for Hannu and then remembered Edgar's request. She reached into her pocketbook and fished out the envelope. She handed Hannu to Robert, tore open the envelope, took out the enclosed sheet of paper and began to read as Robert looked on. She blushed crimson and her color deepened as she read on. Rather than clothing measurements, she was reading an angry, venomous letter from Edgar accusing Robert of trying to seduce his young wife.

"What's the matter?" Robert asked. Mayu didn't answer. The children's clothes section in a department store hardly seemed the proper place for a dialogue about marital fidelity. Now, despite all her hopes, Mayu knew that Robert was doing what she had feared all over again—and if this is his basic nature, she thought, no amount of lecturing is going to change him.

Back at their friend's apartment on Mannerheim Street where they were camping out, Mayu gave Robert the gist of the letter and then read the crucial part. "I want Robert to stay away from my wife. If he will not, I may be forced into drastic measures to stop him."

After a miserable three weeks, they returned to Colombia. Mayu drove down to the Gomez's to retrieve Mishka. She found the poor dog in a sorry state. It would walk rubbing up against the wall, exhibiting symptoms of severe neurosis. Most strangely, Mishka, who had always been affectionate, shunned human company. Confused and concerned, Mayu called Paivi. "What happened to my dog?" she asked.

There was a long silence and then Paivi responded. "Edgar abused the dog when you were in Finland." Mayu didn't have to pursue the matter any further. She could clearly see that Edgar had taken all his hostility and anger for Robert out on the poor helpless animal. Only a sick man, Mayu thought, would punish my dear pet for the sins of his master. At the same time, she understood that Robert had pushed Edgar over the edge. Robert couldn't be so obtuse and insensitive that he couldn't make the connection. Watching the whimpering, cowering dog, Mayu thought that maybe one good thing would come of this disaster: Robert would learn from his mistakes and finally keep his hands to himself.

Though Robert and Mayu were sucked into the orbit of Colombian upper crust social life—late night parties, dancing, visits to ranches in small private planes—they maintained a regimen of work at the office and at home. Robert's doctoral dissertation was still not finished. After dinner, they would go upstairs to the den and settle down to work on it. Late in the evening, they would move from the den to the bedroom. Their work on the dissertation, however, was more harmonious than what would come after.

"What's the matter, Mayu? Your lips are cold and you're completely dry," Robert once said in irritation.

"Give me time," Mayu pleaded, knowing full well that a few minutes later she would not feel any more passionate. This sorry scene played itself out more times than Mayu cared to remember. Robert would then find that he couldn't perform, blaming his momentary impotence on the physical disgust he felt at seeing Mayu's one breast so much smaller than the other.

"You just are not passionate enough," Robert said. "Sex just isn't good between us."

Mayu would turn over to her side and softly weep into her pillow. She would remember the early days of their relationship and marriage when they had had no sexual difficulties and could make love forever in the wilderness, at home, anywhere. Now, it seemed like a nightmare. There was a total sexual impasse between them. Robert's escapades and sexual overtures to other women had a chilling effect on her desire for him. And since Mayu no longer wanted him, Robert found it hard to find fulfillment with her. If only he would realize that he's the one causing the whole problem, she brooded. Her thoughts would begin to whirl, making her dizzy, until sleep rescued her, drawing a curtain of darkness and oblivion over the pain.

****

One night, a party was going full blast. It seemed that every beautiful woman in Bogota was there. But Mayu found herself the object of special attention from the second finance minister, a handsome mulatto, who combined the best qualities of both races. At first, she was taken aback. Then, she was flattered. Robert's affairs had given her self-esteem such a blow that she could not believe that anyone could find her attractive. She was glad that Robert was home with the flu.

"I would be very honored if you would accept my invitation to have lunch with me at my apartment. A quiet lunch…just you and me." The minister spoke softly and with drama, then flashed an irresistible smile.

"I accept with pleasure," Mayu responded. She thought that this was an excellent chance for her to prove to herself that there was nothing wrong with her, and that she could be desired, wanted, by the handsomest of men, holding a high social position.

"I will not be able to sleep until we meet again," the minister said, as they parted. Mayu's thoughts were much the same. She flashed a smile and left, feeling a sensual joy that she hadn't experienced in a long time.

The following day, she slipped out of the house, drove downtown and took a slow elevator up to the fifth-floor apartment, being as careful as possible not to be seen. She briefly remembered how she had told Saku that she never wanted to be a "back-door woman." Then, she shoved the thought out of her mind and followed her desires. When she rang the bell, the door immediately opened, as if the minister had been waiting impatiently for her just behind it. At first glance, she saw that the apartment was tastefully decorated, but she got the odd feeling that nobody lived there. Before she had a chance to take a second look, the man took her to the bedroom, which was dominated by an ornate, circular bed and hung with mirrors all around the walls and ceiling. He was in such a hurry that she had to tell him to take it easy. When he undressed and Mayu saw how shapely his body was and how well-endowed, she didn't want to wait a moment longer. When he took her, she was panting with desire and the feeling was wonderful. But then the unexpected happened—the minister screamed with pleasure and the whole thing was over within a minute. Mayu felt as though she had been doused with cold water. The minister didn't even bother to lie next to her and hold her. Instead, he jumped up and started to get dressed. "How about some lunch?" he asked.

"No, I'm not hungry," Mayu responded in a monotone. She then stared stonily at the ceiling, only to see her brooding face staring back.

That afternoon, she arrived home with a bad taste in her mouth, as well as a feeling of sexual unfulfillment. She rationalized the minister's behavior as a result of his anxiousness; he had been over-stimulated and may have been suffering from "white woman syndrome." Being with a young, fair-skinned Scandinavian blonde must have been the fulfillment of his ultimate sexual fantasy, she thought, and he simply couldn't wait long for the denouement. As her mind churned with thoughts, she did whatever she could to keep the focus off of herself. There was no way she could admit another sexual failure. She decided that, given time, things with the minister would settle down and enjoyment would begin between them. Or would it?

★★★★

Mayu immersed herself in her job. She enjoyed working with Dr. Abdullia Cacores, the director of the project, for his high degree of professionalism and humble, down-to-earth personality. By now, Mayu was fluent in Spanish and the two could talk with great ease. In spite of his advanced medical training, Dr. Cacores sustained an interest in the sometimes numbing details of the nutrition study, which endeared him to Mayu. Like herself, Cacores had risen from humble beginnings. Although his family had been peasants, his education, wealth and position of authority had not turned his head. He continued to dress casually, even sloppily, and slurp his soup as he drank it. But when there was work to be done, Cacores was one of the most thorough men Mayu had ever encountered. He recognized Mayu's ability and instead of being threatened by her, he appreciated her intelligence and offered her warm encouragement. In the ugly skirmishes Mayu had with her co-workers, he came to her rescue and tried to explain her to those who did not understand. When Mayu's marriage was on the rocks and nothing seemed to be going right in her life, she found fulfillment in her work. And Cacores was the one who made it all possible.

But when she developed a problem, it was Helga Eklund, a Swedish psychologist on the project, and not Cacores, to whom she turned. Mayu was pregnant and was uncertain who the father was. One minute, she was convinced it was Robert's baby. The next minute, she was equally convinced that it was the minister's child. She shared her dilemma with Helga.

"Having this baby is absolutely out of the question," Helga said. She added, "There's a 50 percent probability that the child is Robert's. That would be no problem. But there is also a 50 per cent chance that the father is the minister, and if that is the case, then the child's color will speak for itself and there will be serious trouble. If both men were blond, of course, then you could pass the child off as Robert's."

"I could never do that to Robert," Mayu said, indignantly. So there seemed to be only one course of action open and Mayu took it. They secretly found a doctor who could perform an abortion. During the ordeal, Helga stayed with her. Mayu remained at home for a couple of days after the surgery. During her pensive moments, she felt remorse about her affair—not simply because she had gotten pregnant, but because the affair had failed in its purpose of restoring her confidence in herself as a woman. She must have had a half dozen encounters with the minister and each time, he had performed miserably. The whole thing never lasted more than a minute. It became clear to her that she was a novelty and that his desire for her had nothing to do with her as a person. It could have been any white woman. She didn't want to have anything to do with that sort of thing any longer.

****

Robert had always loved music. He would sit in a straight-backed chair and tenaciously practice his tuba, sometimes perfecting one single note for hours on end. One day, on a whim, he went down and auditioned at the Colombian Symphony Orchestra and was hired on the spot. His current job would be no problem, they told him. Soon after that, Robert started staying away from home in the evenings. Though not given to spying on her husband, one evening Mayu needed to reach him. She called the Symphony, only to be told that Robert wasn't there.

"Where were you?" Mayu confronted him when he finally came home late that night. In a rare moment of truth, Robert confessed to her that he had met a young American woman, Cathy, who played oboe in the Symphony. He added that she was "sexually stimulating."

That night, Mayu decided to give the best performance of her life and beat the competition. She gave her husband a sensual massage and he got stimulated. But after a strong start, Robert suddenly stopped and said, "Mayu, you should do lip exercises."

"What do you mean, lip exercises?" Mayu asked, puzzled.

"When you kiss people who play wind instruments, you feel you're really being kissed." Robert didn't have to explain any further. Mayu knew. She went cold. There was no way she could develop a musician's lips. And why should I? she fumed.

The following night, Robert came home late again. He bragged that he was coming from Cathy's bed and that she had been wonderful. Somehow, Mayu fell asleep, but woke in the middle of the night unable to breathe.

Dr. Mondragon, who had come to know Mayu and her marital problems since Hannu's birth, diagnosed stress, gave her Valium and comforted her. It seemed to bring her some temporary relief.

Robert woke Mayu up very early one morning from a deep sleep and announced that he was leaving her and moving in with Cathy. Numb and groggy, Mayu got up, put on her bathrobe and helped Robert load the things he wanted to take along into their Renault. She drove him to Cathy's house and watched as he walked in through the door where the oboist with the sensitive lips was waiting.

Robert was gone. She sat sobbing with her head down on the steering wheel. Hannu, barely four, climbed into the front seat and put his tiny hand on her back. "Don't worry, Mommy. I love you, even if Daddy doesn't."

Sobbing, Mayu turned around and pulled Hannu into her arms. She found great comfort in holding her son.

****

Mayu moved Hannu into her big empty bed to keep her company through the long nights. One morning, two weeks later, the first rays of sun had barely peeked into the house when the noise of something stirring woke Mayu up. She forced her heavy lids open to see what was happening. She blinked her eyes, as she saw Robert standing before her, looking sheepish.

"I made a big mistake, Mayu," he said. "I want you to forgive me and take me back." She released Hannu from her arms and sat up. Her sudden movement startled him. When the child saw Robert, he jumped off the bed, ran up and clung to his father's legs. Robert picked him up and held him tight against his chest. With his apology, along with the emotional reunion of father and son, Mayu didn't see how she could be hard enough to say "no."

"There's an Eastern proverb that the one who returns home in the evening after being lost in the morning was never really lost at all," she said, and stretched out her arms to her husband. With little Hannu in the middle, Mayu and Robert embraced as two long-lost friends. Mayu remembered that her father had also left home, but he had never returned. At least Robert has returned and was penitent. Her hurt and pain were very real, but so was her love for Robert. In spite of everything, that emotion had never changed.

It was a good thing that Robert had decided to come home now. The Colombian project was coming to an end and they were supposed to move on to Boston. Perhaps there, we can begin a new life together and put all of this behind us for good, Mayu said to herself.

CHAPTER EIGHT

1982 Shanni

Washington summers are notoriously cruel. Before air conditioning, European diplomats were given hardship pay to serve in the American capital, built as it was on the steamy, swampy banks of the Potomac. Even now, everyone who can get out of town in the summer, does so. But this year, summer arrived with unprecedented fury. Every time I emerged from my office, I walked amid the skyscrapers that had mushroomed in Rosslyn, just across Key Bridge from the District of Columbia. The Washington building code will not allow skyscrapers, for fear they will dwarf the Washington Monument and the Jefferson Memorial. But no such restrictions exist in the Virginia suburbs. To me, the Rosslyn skyscrapers seem now like very efficient solar heat reflectors. The humid, stagnant air trapped between them is too heavy to rise and too sluggish to stir. A walk through this air is like a walk through a steam bath.

I could have remained indoors and eaten my sandwich in the faculty lounge. It was just that several days had gone by since I'd seen Mayu and I was hoping to run into her outside. I was feeling too proud to pick up the phone and call her. Since we had met back in March, we had been going out regularly. Every single time we went out, I was the one who had initiated the call. But now, I'd reached a point where I felt she should give *me* a call once in a while. So, the days dragged on; I didn't call her and she didn't call me. I wasn't eating or sleeping very well.

As I walked down the skywalk, I was amused to see all the high federal officials and corporate executives stripping off their power suits. Beads of sweat formed on their foreheads, as they scurried back into the coolness of their buildings to eat their lunches away from the oppressive heat. I followed the crowds to the Eatery, thinking how Nature can be a great equalizer. We human beings create all kinds of barriers to set ourselves apart from each other, but in this heat everyone suffers equally.

I remembered how Mayu frowned on the slightest hint that I was trying to set myself above other people. "Seeing you in a three-piece suit," she had told me once, with scarcely-disguised contempt, "makes me itch all over." Well, I had given up wearing three-piece suits—whether to please her or because she had struck a nerve in my conscience, I don't know. She had noted this change in me with great satisfaction. But as to the change I would like to see in her—taking the initiative to call me—well, that was seemingly beyond her power.

The moment I entered the food court, I felt my sweat evaporating in the cool air. There were a dozen stalls and deciding on what kind of food to get was not an easy choice. A blended fruit and ice drink seemed like an antidote to this weather. To fortify myself for the half-day of teaching that was still ahead of me, I asked the Greek woman behind the counter for a plate of moussaka. I asked her what the ingredients were. She didn't know, she said, and gave me a suspicious look that clearly said she thought I was trying to pick her up. "Just philosophic curiosity," I added, with a sad smile, and walked away, wondering why we are all so suspicious of each other's motives.

Holding my tray, I swung around and scanned the packed seating area, hoping against hope that Mayu would be in the throng. I came out of the building to the skywalk level and saw a few hardy souls eating at the benches and outdoor tables. I walked up to the last table, which was right in the line of sight of anyone coming from the annex building where Mayu worked. I sat down, facing away from the path so my intentions would not be so conspicuous. I didn't bother to remove the food from the red plastic tray. Instead, I unfolded the *New York Times* that I had bought from a newspaper box. I tried to read an article, but my eyes wouldn't focus. I choked on my first bite of the sandwich and gulped down some of the fruit drink to clear the obstruction. Clearly, my mind was not on the traumas of my body, but on the sound of every footstep as it first became audible in the distance. As each person passed, I would cast a side-long glance, but each time I was disappointed. Having given up on seeing Mayu, I don't know at what point I actually finished my lunch, but I was in the middle of an article on the Iran-Iraq war when that familiar voice startled me.

"So! You made sure I wouldn't miss you." I turned around and there she was, with a broad smile, wearing a familiar polka-dot dress that was one of her favorites.

"Imagine meeting you here," I said nonchalantly, as if that were the farthest thing from my mind.

"Uh-huh," she responded, sarcastically. "Now tell me the truth. You seated yourself right there, so I wouldn't miss you."

I simply laughed, a high-pitched, self-conscious giggle that betrayed the truth. Where we were, there was a constant stream of people, many of them administrators and lecturers with whom we worked, and I did n't feel comfortable showing affection for Mayu in front of them. I got up and we both started walking down the skywalk to a tiny matchbox-sized park that served to relieve the harshness of the concrete. Still, we were not alone. There were others there for purposes less lofty than love: eating sandwiches and taking naps, braving the sun which was at its zenith.

Looking into my eyes, Mayu said, "I would have come earlier, except that I decided to eat the smoked herring and fruit I brought from home first. I was very hungry." Then, squeezing my hand, she added, "I was hoping to run into you."

I don't know what got into me at that point. I felt my eyes ablaze and the words escaped my mouth like steam from an overheated radiator. "I'm not going to initiate our phone calls every single time, even if an eternity goes by and I feel like I'm dying."

She was taken aback with the intensity of my feeling. She put her arms around me and gently kissed me on the lips. Then, she rubbed her nose on mine, moving her head from side to side, looking into my eyes sideways. I felt calmed as she embraced me. When we parted from the embrace, it felt like we were alone in the park. In fact, it had largely emptied and now the predominant sound was the persistent traffic on the street leading to Washington.

"Oh my God!" I said, looking at my watch, "we're late for work."

As we prepared to return, Mayu said, "We're both invited for dinner at the Hancocks's on Friday night. Can you make it?"

"Yes," I said.

"Come to my house around 6:00," Mayu said. She gave me a searching look, as though she were trying to assure herself that she had completely placated my anger, then hurried away.

****

"George Hancock also worked on the Bogota project," Mayu told me, as I drove her and her nine-year-old second son, Esko, to our dinner engagement. She went on, "But he tried so hard to please everybody that one could never be sure where he stood. Sometimes, he could be on both sides of an issue. It was so pathetic. I thought he was a wimp and never liked him."

Then why are we socializing with him, if you don't like him? I thought, but didn't voice my question.

"He has changed so much since then. Really, it's unbelievable," she said, as if reading my thoughts.

"I find it helpful," I said, "if I get a briefing on a person in chronological order...where a person was born, what he did with his life and when he died. That sort of thing helps me get a fix on a person."

"He's not dead yet," she said, laughing. "George Hancock," she went on, "had a most unusual background. His father was an emigré from the Basque region of Spain and his mother was Russian. They settled in New York City and, nine years later, George was born. As soon as they could, they packed him off to boarding schools in Argentina and Chile. It's not clear to me why his parents wanted to be rid of him, except perhaps to give him a Latin education. But one thing is clear...living with strangers had a very unsalutary psychological effect on him. He learned to please everybody and grew a stranger to himself.

"That was his problem in Colombia. He was never his own man. Being a toady worked well for a while—everybody was happy with him—but then he was found out and people began to take what he had to say with a grain of salt. It was really sad because he was a brilliant man with a Ph.D. in anthropology from Berkeley.

"He was married twice before meeting Angela, a Colombian lawyer and socialite. I don't know how it was in his previous marriages, but in this one George certainly did a lot of accommodating. A change came over him after they came back to this country to live. He seemed to come into his own. He and Angela moved to Kalamazoo, where he got a job with the Board of Education. Angela, though, was miserable in a small Midwestern town.

"George worked for ten years out there before landing a Congressional internship. That's when they moved to this area. They bought a condo in Fairfax and decorated it in a Scandinavian style. Angela had always wanted a stage for her considerable talents and it seemed that she found it here. She got more svelte every day, took evening classes at Georgetown University, dressed in designer dresses bought at Bloomingdale's and Neiman-Marcus and floated around like a blissful butterfly. George also found many outlets for his intellectual growth.

"You turn off here," Mayu said. "The rest of the family history you can find out for yourself."

It was George who answered the doorbell and welcomed Mayu with a hug and a kiss on the cheek. As we entered further into the house, I was introduced. Both George and Angela said, "We've heard so much about you!"

"I'll take that as a compliment," I said.

Mayu was right. The house did have a Scandinavian rather than a Latin ambiance. It also struck me that Angela answered in English every time Mayu spoke to her in Spanish. There seemed to be some kind of undercurrent at work that I didn't understand. As I sat down on the cream-colored leather couch, I was impressed by the number of plants and how lush they were. The living room was at a right angle to the dining room and the corner where the two met looked like a little conservatory, with a skylight above. The two young Hancock children, Sonia and Jose, appeared briefly. Esko, who had been telling us during the ride over that he didn't really like Jose, went off with them.

While I was taking everything in, Mayu and George were deep in conversation. Some of it I understood, but most I did not.

They were talking about statistical analysis, a subject that I had successfully avoided during my graduate school days. Shut out, Angela and I were looking at each other, forcing smiles. Alternately, we would look at George and Mayu and wonder how long they would go on talking and ignoring us. Angela finally lit a cigarette and started puffing. I, not being a smoker, awkwardly attempted a conversation. It was a painful effort for me to draw her out. I probably would have been better off just sitting quietly or daydreaming. But it was too late now.

I was bleeding inside, seeing George and Mayu so absorbed in each other. Since I came from a culture where women wear veils and live segregated from men, such intimate contact between men and women not married to one another never failed to shock me. Here I was, stranded with a stranger on the outskirts of the animated conversation that my girlfriend was conducting with the stranger's husband. Mayu made no attempt to include either Angela or me. In fact, she seemed utterly unaware that we were even present.

Coincidentally, the lively interchange between Mayu and George, and my halting dialogue with Angela, paused at the same moment. Suddenly, the room was still. Angela broke the silence, "It never fails. Every time George and Mayu get together, they sit in a corner and talk...and they can talk forever."

I asked, "You don't think that there's anything between them?"

Hearing these words, Mayu jumped in and answered. "Of course there is. There's a lot between us." While I understood the import of Mayu's defensive comment, Angela became rather melancholic and began to reminisce.

"I used to be so jealous of Mayu in Bogota. She was blonde and pretty, and so self-assured. She could talk both in English and Spanish. Every time she would talk to George, I would feel bad. It was not just George who liked to talk to her...all the men vied for her attention."

"This is news to me," Mayu said. George smiled neutrally. I didn't say anything, although I was amazed at how Angela's assessment of Mayu as pretty and self-assured was diametrically opposed to Mayu's own self-image during that time in Colombia.

At just that moment, the oven timer sounded. "Oh," said Angela, as though coming out of a trance, "dinner is ready." To my surprise, Angela served a goose. It also surprised me that it was not George, but Angela who sliced the goose into pieces with a thin, very sharp knife and placed them on a Wedgewood plate to be passed around the table.

As the dinner progressed, I had a chance to hear George talk, though Mayu, in her inimitable way, was still dominating the conversation. She had accurately described him as brilliant, I thought. I was impressed by his clarity of thought and lucidity of expression. He had the knack of timing, saying the right thing at the right time. He put me somewhat at ease, which helped assuage my hurt feelings.

When we were in the midst of eating dessert, Esko appeared and informed Mayu that he and Jose were not getting along and that he was ready to go home. I was relieved when we left almost immediately.

I was still feeling resentment at the warmth between Mayu and George, although my irritation was not evident enough for Mayu to notice. Even that bothered me. If she were really tuned into my feelings, I reasoned, she would pick up on even the most subtle of my mood changes. But she seemed lost in a room of warm thoughts with a *Keep Out* sign on the door.

At the house, Mayu left me in the living room and went inside, as she put it, to tuck Esko in. He slept in her big double bed. She was gone a long time and I whiled away the time patting Mayu's big, affectionate dog, Gypsy, while turning over the events of the evening in my mind.

When Mayu finally returned, she said, "We should go dancing some time." I was taken aback by this non sequitur, although by now, I should have been used to her mind darting from thought to thought.

"Any time you like." I smiled. "We could go tomorrow."

"Great!" she said enthusiastically, and then asked whether I was going to stay or leave. For a moment, I didn't know how to answer, but then I decided I should tell her how I felt.

"I could stay, but it troubles me to sleep with you in the same bed where Esko is sleeping."

"In that case, let's go down to the rec room." We went downstairs and Gypsy followed. Mayu threw the cushions off the two little couches—even in the dim light, I could see they were frayed and matted with dog hair—and arranged them together on the floor. It hurt my sensibility, but I decided to bear it. We lay down, she wearing her robe and I my underclothes. Under me, I could feel the gap between the cushions. I would have liked to say, "Alone at last!" except we were not alone. The dog was constantly trying to make it a threesome. Mayu was on one side, and the dog was on the other, breathing down my neck.

"In bed, at last!" I amended, with just enough sarcasm for Mayu to pick up on my mood.

"Any criticism of our visit to the Haycocks?"

I felt a surge of anger. "Yeah, only that you ignored me all evening and spent the whole time talking to George. Is that the way you used to act with Robert? Look, I don't want you to cast me as Robert when you re-enact scenes from your defunct marriage."

Although it was too dark to see her clearly, I could see that my comment had had quite an impact on her. She was staring toward the ceiling pensively. I firmly pushed the dog away and it finally got the message. Mayu said nothing, and the silence was punctuated only by the dog's breathing. Unable to bear it any more, I said, "What is it, Mayu?"

"You touched a raw nerve, that's all."

"I'm sorry."

"No...no...there was a lot in truth in what you said. In a way, you opened my eyes. I can see that I'm approaching this relationship with preconceived notions."

"That's not fair to either of us."

"No matter how free we want to be, we remain prisoners of the past."

"Not necessarily," I pleaded. "And not all of us. Some of us, to use a cliché, rise above it all. Through growth and regeneration, we shed the old skin which doesn't fit us anymore and live in the here and now."

Mayu reflected. "Wise words, but it's not easy for me to change, just like that, the feelings I have for men because of Robert." She smiled wryly and added, "Maybe, instead of 'feelings,' I should have said 'lack of feelings.'"

"How long were you married to him?"

"Thirteen years," she told me. "You know, on the one hand, Robert always admired the way I discussed issues in a social situation. On the other hand, he would always criticize me for getting carried away by those very discussions. If I could only be a middle-of-the-road person, he used to say, social get-togethers would be so much more fun."

I thought guiltily that I rather agreed with Robert.

She continued, "This change, this transformation on his part from tolerance to criticism, was so ironic. I mean, what a turncoat! I've told you before that I had always wanted to find a cause worth dying for. I was hopeful that Robert would help me in finding one, or if I did find one, he would support me in it.

"There was one more area where I thought Robert could be helpful. Since I came from a poor family, I thought Robert could help me develop social graces. But it didn't work like that; he just criticized me, and most of the time for the same things he used to admire in me."

"People do change," I told her, "and they should. Life wouldn't be natural, otherwise."

"But he didn't really change," she insisted. "He just came full circle. He returned to his roots, to the values that his parents had spoon-fed him. I was just an interloper in his life; deep down he was always itching to get back to his parents' conservatism. Emotional hardening of the arteries sanctioned by tradition, and bigotry sanctioned by religion." Mayu stopped talking. This was the second time we were in bed together with Mayu crying.

The following night, I picked her up and we drove downtown to my favorite Pakistani restaurant, Shezan. I was a regular there. Its manager was an older woman with an unusual background; her mother was half-Irish, half-Pakistani. She was always at the restaurant, presiding over a round table surrounded by her acquaintances. The hostess was a pretty, slender Anglo-Indian lady with a ready smile, who always greeted me by name and gave me a good table. No sooner would I be seated when the two waiters, Carter and Jeremiah, would come and vie with each other to serve me. Carter and I had a running joke; when I was finished eating and he would come to sweep the crumbs off the table, he would tell me that the mess of crumbs meant that I must have enjoyed the food. The food *was* good, as a matter of fact, and the restaurant was a sort of home away from home for me.

But today, as Mayu and I walked down the narrow steps, I didn't see the hostess's familiar face. A strange-sounding man with a raspy voice seated us. When an equally strange person showed up at the table to take our order, I asked about the people I had known.

"The restaurant has been sold," he told me. "We have a new management." The words were said in an emotionless monotone, so I knew that this man had not known and loved the previous restaurant staff as I had. He also told me that the big husky man who was walking around awkwardly was the new manager. My heart sank. Oblivious to my feelings, Mayu was admiring the brass fittings on the ceiling and the reproductions of Moghul art and tapestries on the walls. Mayu asked me to help with the menu, so I ordered for both of us. The food wasn't bad at all, but I kept getting strange feelings about the service. The promptness, the caring and the finesse of Carter and Jeremiah were missing. Maybe, I thought, my feelings are hurt because I'm not getting the special attention that I've become so accustomed to at Shezan? A distinct feeling of irritation took hold of me.

"This chicken is quite good. Not too spicy at all," Mayu said, swallowing the last morsel.

"Cooking over an open fire helps. It removes all the excess spices and fat," I responded, trying to sound as pleasant as I could under the circumstances.

"What's that foil?" Mayu asked suspiciously, pointing to the thin silvery coating on the kheer pudding, as the waiter put down our dessert dishes. I explained that pure silver was pounded for hours until it was thinner than the thinnest tissue, then put on desserts. The practice started in Moghul kitchens—both because it was decorative and because it was believed that gold and silver were good for the body. The silver foil had no taste.

Touching the silver foil with a look of uncertainty, Mayu took a tiny bite of the kheer and decided that she didn't like it. "I think I'll just have a coffee now," she said. But the waiter had left without asking whether we wanted tea or coffee, vanishing somewhere into the back. I looked around and realized how desolate the place looked. Most of the tables were empty. There were only a few customers. The manager, the big-boned man with the balding head, was hanging around as useless as a second thumb. I called him over and registered with him my disappointment with the new management. Mayu didn't know exactly what was transpiring since we were speaking Urdu, but she could certainly see that I was on the offensive and he on the defensive. In a few minutes, some other restaurant workers, including the idle bartender, came out to listen to what was being said. The group looked like a class being taken to task by an irate schoolmaster.

When we came out of the restaurant, I explained to Mayu what had happened. She sided immediately with the workers there. "Okay, I'll agree that the service was not the best, but you didn't have to be so harsh," she told me hotly.

I was flabbergasted at this kind of response from her. For several moments, I couldn't recover my composure. I didn't talk to her, as we walked the two blocks to the car. I thought I would take her out dancing; maybe that would help alleviate some of the tension between us? Mayu was still preoccupied with what had happened at the restaurant. Her body was radiating outrage. I remembered she told me once that her mother used to say, "Mayu, if you don't say what's on your mind in words, it will come out through your ribs." Sure enough, she was breathing heavily.

When she finally spoke, she said, "My mother used to cook for the executives in a bank. If those people had been hard on my mother because of some minor slip-up, I would've been furious."

I didn't say anything. I knew nothing would help at this point. But why did I have to put up with this? I thought we were trying to have an enjoyable evening out? I didn't understand why she was turning a restaurant management problem into an ideological problem and a quarrel between us. Considering it was a matter between me and the restaurant, she could have left the whole thing alone. After all, it was her coffee that had triggered my anger to begin with. We were now in the car and I was looking for a parking space. I finally found a small one, but big enough for my little Tercel.

"What?" she asked.

"Come," I said lightly, determined to change the tone of the evening. "We're going to trip the light fantastic. You look like a lady who likes to imagine, now and then, that she's Ginger Rogers." I put my arm around her.

As if she had been resurrected, her face was suddenly animated. "I just love dancing!" We walked into the club. The bouncers scanned our clothes very carefully as we passed them, looking for clues to our characters, but we apparently passed muster because their expressions changed from caution to satisfaction. In the large front room, people were sitting around, drinking. We had to go through a couple of dim rooms before we arrived at the area serving both as bar and dance floor. There were not many people there.

We walked up to the bar where Mayu ordered a Chablis. I never really enjoyed alcohol, although I had accepted cloudberry liqueur from Mayu out of politeness from time to time. I asked the bartender if he could make a fruit punch for me. When he gave me a puzzled look, I said, "Mix orange juice, pineapple juice and any other juice you have, and put in a lemon twist." We had had just a couple of sips of our drinks when the music for a tango came on.

"Let's do this," I said to Mayu. I had taken dance lessons and when we were on the floor, I brought to bear my entire training at the Arthur Murray school.

As I led her into the promenade, she said to me: "You dance very well."

"Certain dances," I said, "but my biggest problem is not being able to hear the beat on a consistent basis." I was sorry to hear the tango end and the music change. What dance could you do to this frantic music? As we walked back to the bar where our drinks were waiting, a short black man, not more than 5'3', with a goatee, wearing a red plaid shirt and frayed, faded blue jeans, approached Mayu.

"Hello. How are you?" As he spoke with deliberate effort, I could tell English wasn't his first language.

"Fine," Mayu responded.

"How 'bout we dance?"

"Sure," she said. Throwing a neutral glance in my general direction, she returned to the dance floor with him. The music had changed twice and when Mayu did not return, I looked over my drink in the direction of the dance floor and spotted them behind several couples, in the farthest corner. From what I could see, the man's hands were on her hips and they were dancing slowly and provocatively. I could not bear it. I turned away and gulped down my punch, as though it were some kind of alcohol that would drown my discomfort.

I think it was Mayu's voice that made me turn around and look. The man was still with her. Rather than thanking Mayu for the dance and walking away, he situated himself between her and me along the bar rail, ordered a drink and tried to engage her in some small talk. When he reached out and tried to shake hands with me, I couldn't take it any more. I pointedly did not extend my hand. Mayu glared furiously at me and started to walk out of the bar. What could I do but get up and follow her?

On her way out, she almost walked into another black man who was standing with a cocktail in his hand. "That looks good," she said. She reached out, took the drink from his hand, downed several sips from it, returned it to him and continued walking toward the exit. It would be hard to say who was more surprised by her action—the man or me. After a moment's shock, he broke into a smile. But as I followed Mayu through the door, my fury mounted. We reached the car in total silence. We were all the way over the bridge in Virginia when Mayu leaned over and, looking into my face, raised and contracted her eyebrows, asking me what the matter was without saying a word. If she didn't know, I wasn't going to tell her. There was a sea of anger raging within me. I kept thinking, what is the *matter* with this woman? But I didn't want to have a confrontation with her. I pretended to concentrate on driving.

"Should I exit onto Route 495 North or South?" I asked. I didn't get an answer. "Well?"

"What do you think?" she asked, in a slow, acid drawl. It was as if she were talking to a backward child. I didn't say anything. Of course I knew that I needed to take 495 South to get to her house. As we got closer to the house, I felt relieved. We passed all the familiar landmarks—the Texaco station, the 7-Eleven. Soon, this agony of driving her home would be over.

When I finally pulled into her driveway, we sat for what seemed like an eternity in cold silence. She continued to play the same old game—leaning down and looking up into my face. All kinds of thoughts were bubbling in the cauldron of my mind. First of all, she was *my* date, I fumed in silence, and I was the one who had taken her dancing. It gave me some rights over her, certainly for the evening. I thought she was supposed to dance with me and me alone. Or even if she agreed to dance with another man, she should not to have encouraged him to paw her all over, or let him get between us and devote the whole evening to exploiting the situation. And then, what was this, grabbing a drink from a total stranger and gulping down her fill? And why had she walked out of the nightclub as if *I* were the one who had done something wrong? I didn't see why I had to shake hands with the man who was insinuating himself into our evening. Under the circumstances, I thought that had been a pretty restrained response. We seemed at an impasse, so she opened the door and walked into the house alone.

I couldn't sleep well that night. As I often did at the end of the day, I tried to make sense of what had happened. I wondered about Mayu's attraction to black men. Maybe, I thought, it has something to do with her liberal philosophy, her family background, her concern for the common man? Maybe this is her, how can I say it, biological way of expressing her freedom from prejudice? If that's the case, then what upset me should maybe, in fact, be admired in her? After all, if she didn't have an open attitude, she wouldn't be seeing me, since I'm Asian. But then why had she gotten upset with me? Perhaps the answer lies in my being solidly middle class? That might have triggered her irascibility. And one must never forget, I thought as I reached for a Sominex on the night table, that cultural and social differences can cause havoc between two people who might otherwise find pleasure in each other's company. It's my duty, I thought, to accept this reality. After all, I suppose loving a woman means more than making her conform to your romantic ideal; it means accepting her as she is—and accepting that conflicts are an inevitable part of love. Resigned to this thought, I slipped into a deep and dreamless sleep.

CHAPTER NINE

1985 Shanni

I had dozed off reading in my reclining chair in the air-conditioned room when the shrill ring of the telephone woke me. I picked up the receiver and fumbled it to the floor until finally bringing it to my ear. There was the familiar voice.

"Robert is being a real bastard. He's threatening to remove his name from the mortgage of the house, if I don't agree to void the pension clause. If I lose the house, no bank will lend me the money for another one. I don't know what to do." I heard the words, though the Finnish accent had become thicker and the words were squeezed out through intermittent sobs.

It took me a few seconds to make the transition from sleep to alertness, so I could focus on Mayu's most recent problem. Even fully awake, though, I didn't have a grasp of the significance of her words. She had a habit of jumping right into the middle of an issue without creating a context. "Mayu," I said, "I'm sorry he's doing this to you, but if you'd give me more details I'd be able to understand your problem a little better." She put a brake on her crying and I could understand her more clearly.

"In the divorce settlement," she told me, "it was agreed that our house, where Hannu, Esko and I still live, would be put up for sale. Later, I got Robert to agree not to sell the house after all, because my low income wouldn't qualify me to buy a new one. Robert also agreed to leave his name on the house's mortgage, since it was his income that enabled me to hold onto it. But now, he's changed his mind again. He's threatening to remove his name from the mortgage unless I agree to relinquish my claim on a quarter of his pension. I'm afraid if he does that, I'll lose the house."

"What is this claim on a quarter of his pension, Mayu?" I asked.

There was a pause. "As you know, I have a deep-seated need for security, so when we were drafting the divorce settlement, I asked my lawyer to write down that if I stayed in the United States and didn't have my own pension, I would get a quarter of Robert's. He agreed to the pension clause at the time of the settlement, but now he wants it removed."

I thought to myself, Mayu is only 40. It will be at least another 25 years before she'll need a pension. That ought to be enough time to generate her own income and pension plan. She was an intelligent, well-educated person. I almost told her this, but thought better of it. I knew that my comments would upset her more than they would help. Since her need was emotional rather than rational, I thought that this was a time for commiseration and not advice.

"I'm sorry he's putting you through this. Let me come over and be with you."

"See you," she said, and hung up.

When I arrived at her house, she was eating. Food was always a source of comfort for her when she was upset. I walked into the house without knocking at the door, which was kept unlocked. She seemed slightly embarrassed at having been caught in the act. Her hair was disheveled and her eyes swollen. I embraced her and kissed her lips, brushing away the crumbs of food that clung there. The smell of smoked turkey surrounded her like perfume.

She and I were still kissing when Esko burst into the kitchen shouting, "Mom, Hannu got me all wet! And my bed is all soaked. Where am I supposed to sleep?"

I laughed and said, "That sounds pretty funny. Since when is Hannu wetting your bed?"

The anger which momentarily had flushed Mayu's cheeks subsided. "What are you complaining about? You don't sleep in your own bed anyway," she said to Esko, without disengaging herself from me. Then she asked if I would like a cup of tea.

I said, "You know I never turn down a cup of tea."

"Go sit down in the living room. I'll put the kettle on and finish cleaning the kitchen." There was a stack of Finnish magazines on the coffee table. I picked one up and began to look at the photos. She called from the kitchen, "Do me a favor."

"What, Mayu?"

"Kill this damn dog." I looked up and there was Gypsy, innocently sauntering out of the kitchen. But then my senses were assailed by the smell of urine.

"I see what you mean. How long have you had Gypsy?"

"Since she was a puppy."

"How come she's not housebroken?"

"This is one of those unsolved mysteries. If it weren't for the boys, I'd get rid of her in a minute." Mayu shouted at the top of her voice, "Hannu, clean your room."

He shouted back at the same decibel level, "I'm going to a party. I'll clean it up tomorrow."

"No. You can't go until you clean."

Hannu came to the kitchen and they argued for a while. I could hear their voices rising. Then there was a lull. When Mayu brought the tea, I whispered, "Why don't you compromise with him? Let him clean a little now, and then let him go to the party on the condition that he finishes the rest first thing tomorrow."

"No, no," she said, shaking her head vehemently, and went back into the kitchen. A few moments later, I heard her shout, "Straighten the room a little now and then go to the party. Be sure to finish it tomorrow."

"I will," replied Hannu from his room. I smiled to myself at my successful diplomacy. Mayu was, of course, too proud to admit that she had taken my advice, but that didn't diminish my pleasure. She returned to the living room and we talked some more about the mortgage and her claim on the pension. Gradually, she began to notice the silence throughout the house.

"I wonder if Hannu has left?" Mayu questioned, taking a quick look at her watch. She got up and went to his room. I heard her groan. I immediately suspected that the straightening of the room had not been done. Mayu returned to confirm my suspicion.

"Why can't number one son be like number two? Hannu gives me a fight every step of the way, while I have such an easy time with Esko." After she posed the question, she sat down next to me. She focused her sunken bluish-gray eyes on my face. It seemed she was asking me to come up with a way to magically transform Hannu and make him more like his brother.

"Just give him time. He's going through a phase right now. He'll outgrow it," I said calmly and took the last sip of my tea.

"No, but he's so different from me and Esko. He lives at such a tempo that he makes me dizzy. He can't even sit down for a second without twitching or tapping his foot. Esko is a typical Finn, like me—he moves almost in slow motion. I have no problem at all dealing with him."

The dog had fallen asleep on my feet. Ever since summer began, she'd hated to go outside, remaining mostly indoors in the air-conditioning. This probably explained why she'd had her accident. Still, she shed everywhere and dog-hair was always flying up and clinging mercilessly to my clothes. Mayu and I had agreed that these hot Washington summers must be hell for a Siberian husky. At this moment, though, Gypsy looked quite contented.

"So, regarding this mortgage..." I said, inviting Mayu to return to our previous subject.

"We bought this house when we came to Washington from Sweden in 1981," Mayu began.

"It's never been clear to me why you went to live in Sweden in the first place," I interrupted her.

"Well, we made the decision standing outside my cabin on Lake Saima in Finland, enjoying the summer weather. That was after we'd been in Boston for a year." She knit her brows, as she always did when she was pensive. "Coping with the Harvard community was tough for us. We never really fit into that closed world of East Coast preppies. And both of us hated the director of the Cambridge phase of the project. We thought it would be a shame to go back to that misery. So, as we were looking out at the lake and enjoying the serenity, we decided to stay in Scandinavia. On reflection, it didn't seem fair to Robert to settle in Finland. That would give me a linguistic and cultural advantage over him."

"What do you mean?" I asked.

"Well," sighed Mayu, "we'd all like to believe that love conquers all and that things like that wouldn't matter. But I knew when I was living in the States just how out of place a person can feel in a foreign land. And I guess I thought that if one of us was going to be a stranger in the land, then both of us should be."

I smiled at her original logic and motioned for her to continue.

"Anyway," she said, "we thought we should live in a country where neither of us would have the advantage. We figured we could live in Sweden. Robert went to Stockholm and walked right into the National Bureau of Music—he has even more gall than I do!—to audition as a tuba player. He got the job right away. He was lucky and that sort of thing happened a lot in his life.

"They gave him a choice of three places, one of them being Boden in the north, above the Arctic Circle. He called me…I had gone to Lahti…and I suggested Boden was the place we should choose. That summer, we must have made half a dozen trips from Finland to Sweden in our old Peugeot. We bought a house six kilometers out of town and settled down in Arctic serenity with the boys. Hannu was six then and Esko was only one-and-a-half.

"Robert would practice his tuba for hours on end outside in the limitless expanse of the Nordic wilderness. I whiled away my time taking care of the children, puttering around the house, growing vegetables, and knitting. Sometimes, the loneliness of it crept into my bones and became very oppressive.

"The monotony of life was broken by pleasant events, like a visit from my old friend from Minnesota, David Howard, and his family. There were also unpleasant ones, like the time Robert was sued by a Swedish musician who claimed that Robert's orchestra job should have gone to a Swede. Then there was the time that Robert came home with a 20-year old Finnish girl, a violinist in the orchestra. It was obvious that they had just been in bed together. Still, all of us sat down to dinner around our table. I was struck by the absurdity of the situation...three adults, each knowing that the others knew exactly what was going on, but no one saying a word, just eating Swedish meatballs as though nothing were out of the ordinary.

"For a year, I went around being Mayu Larsen, hiding my Finnishness, knowing that my Swedish neighbors would treat me like a second-class citizen, if they knew I was Finnish. That, unfortunately, is the legacy of Swedish domination of Finland for 600 years.

"One morning, I got up and decided to announce to the neighbors that I was Mayu Kaariainen before my marriage. I came out of the closet, as it were. I became active in the Finnish community and even took a job as a psychologist working with the many Finns there in Sweden.

"Robert subscribed to the *International Herald Tribune* out of Paris and, at one point, decided to answer an ad placed in it by the Nestle Corporation, which was looking for a representative in Washington, D.C. He applied for the job but was not accepted right away. Nestle wrote him to say that, although they found his credentials impressive—his experience on the Harvard project especially caught their eye—they were really interested in someone with a background in physiology. However, that was not their definitive answer to him. They indicated that they might be in touch. Months passed. Robert, quite naturally, assumed that another applicant had been selected for the position. One morning, he found a letter in the mail, and to his great surprise, as well as mine, it was Nestle asking Robert to come to Geneva to be interviewed. He flew to Geneva and was hired before he even left the interview room. He was delighted, but I had some misgivings about leaving Scandinavia and moving to the United States.

"'You go to Washington,' I said to Robert, 'and see how you like your work. Get a feel of the city as a place to live and raise children. We can make the decision about moving as a family later.'

"That was in 1981. So, Robert moved to Washington by himself. Right after he started at Nestle, he had an incredible stroke of luck. The man sitting next to him on a plane happened to be the leader of the movement for boycotting Nestle over its sales of baby formula to the Third World. The boycott was costing Nestle millions of dollars a year. Somehow, Robert convinced the man of Nestle's innocence and he agreed to call off the boycott. It meant a huge bonus and pay raise for Robert, and he was virtually assured of a secure position with Nestle as long as he wanted one.

"I would have looked a fool if I resisted joining him." Mayu sighed. "We had been corresponding and talking on the phone. Finally I told him, against my better judgment, that yes, I would join him with the children, so he should go ahead and find a place for us to live. He found this house in the neighborhood called Emerson Woods. The vacancy coincided with our arrival. As soon as I came with the children, we moved right in. It's a good house with lots of room and we've enjoyed it. I'm hoping to rent out the guest room to a student, if I can get it fixed up. It's a good neighborhood, too. There's a community pool and a trail where I like to walk Gypsy..." Mayu's voice trailed off.

"I guess you're remembering your first days in the house when you were still married," I said.

"Yeah," she said, bitterly. "I don't know what I'm going to do. I can't lose this house."

"I don't know what to suggest, Mayu," I said. "But I'm sure it must be very upsetting. Can I ask you something? If your marriage survived Minneapolis, Copenhagen, Bogota, Cambridge, and Boden, how come it collapsed in Washington?"

"In other cities, we had problems in our marriage because Robert couldn't keep his pants zipped. In Washington, the problem became much more complicated. Here, he became a corporate executive and reverted into a Republican, while I became an impediment to his aspirations of upward mobility. Back in 1969, when Robert and I first met, university campuses were like a brave new world unto themselves. The older generation who grew up in the Depression aspired to a secure middle-class life...a home in the suburbs with a two-car garage and periodic cookouts. They wanted to give their children everything they had been denied themselves. But when these children came of age in the 60's, they rejected the values of their parents and questioned the Establishment. Robert got sucked into the vortex of this storm almost in spite of himself.

He grew long hair, wore cut-offs, got high on grass and acid, and reveled in free love. But, as it turns out, he was just going along with the crowd...conforming with the non-conformists, trying to fit in!

"By 1981, when he arrived in Washington, Reagan was in office. A conservative wind was blowing and Robert pulled off his chameleon act one more time. Robert, the hippie, shed the liberalism of the 60's and...Poof!...miraculously changed into Robert, the conservative smooth operator of the 80's.

"The real test of our marriage on the ideological level came when he wanted me to go with him to the White House dinner. I turned him down. I could see how disappointed he was. It put tremendous stress on our marriage. When we were at the opera that night, the tension between us was so great that you could almost touch it. A leftist wife might be an asset on a campus, but in the business world, she could ruin the career of an executive husband."

"So," I observed, "he left you for being what you have always been and he had always known you were."

"Not just that. As I told you before, it was for not providing him with 'good sex,' as well. I couldn't stand the way he'd expect me to get turned on by his jumping from some other woman's bed into mine. Speaking of which, let's go to bed now."

By this time, I was too used to Mayu's abrupt shifts in mood to be surprised.

When we entered the bedroom, Mayu said, "Well, Esko's here. The three of us will have to sleep together. I suppose we can all fit here. You know, when Robert found out that Esko sleeps in my bed, he implied that I was giving him some sort of Oedipus complex."

I said, "I don't know about that. I remember I liked to snuggle against my mother until I was a teenager."

"It's just like Robert," said Mayu, "to see problems where none exist." She straightened the sheets with a complaint that she could never find the right size of sheet for the Finnish mattress. She added: "I'll sleep in the middle to keep the males apart." There was a mischievous glint in her eye, as though she knew how sensitive men could get at the mere suggestion of intimacy with another male. As we lay side by side on the bed, she kept looking at the luminous numbers on the clock on the bedside table. It was after 1:00 a.m. and she was worried because Hannu was still not home.

"A delay doesn't necessarily mean he's in trouble," I said. "If I remember from my own boyhood, looking at the clock is the last thing teenagers do when they're having a good time." She kissed me, and though I couldn't see her face, I could sense that she was reassured. Her hand began to roam over my body. I couldn't forget that a child was lying just on the other side—I could hear his breathing—but she was exciting me, and I thought that as weird as it was for me, if this arrangement was okay with her, perhaps I ought not to object. We got underway and then we both heard the sound of the front door closing.

"Oh! Hannu's home. I have to see what shape he's in." She pushed me off her. I lay on my back, out of breath and slightly dazed. She got up and, stark naked, walked out of the darkness of the bedroom and into the bright light of the hallway. "Hannu, where have you been? It's two o'clock."

"Mo-om, don't shout like that. I've got ears." Esko stirred and turned on his side, as one loud voice and another, not so loud, resounded just outside the door. Mayu was accusing Hannu of having taken drugs, and Hannu was denying it.

"But you look stoned. Look at you, you can hardly walk!" she shouted. I heard the sound of a couple of smacks, followed by Hannu's subdued "Ow!" I was sure he knew I was in the bedroom and that his mother had gone from me to confront him. She walked back into the bedroom, saying over her shoulder, "You do that again and I'll ground you." She didn't bother to close the door behind her and I could see her expression in the light from the hallway. It was the distraught face of a mother at the end of her rope.

"I'm taking them to Finland. I'm not going to raise my children in America," she said, climbing into bed, jostling Esko and me until she plopped herself down.

"Teenagers experiment with different things," I said, soothingly. "It's part of growing up. If parents are patient and understanding, they can get themselves and their kids through this period in one piece."

"Where were we?" she asked me in a sexy voice. We somehow picked up where we had left off. Afterwards, as our breathing slowed to normal, we both heard the sound of Esko sobbing. We realized simultaneously what must have happened. Neither of us thought that he would wake up with our noise when he seemed to have slept through Hannu's return. I put my robe on and left the room, so Mayu could deal with the situation. Several minutes later, she joined me in the living room and said, "He's very upset that we were making love while he was right there in the bed. Actually, he was awake through the whole thing."

I felt sick. I said, "We used to go to one extreme, making love in the rec room after the kids had gone to sleep and trying to hide all the evidence, and now we have gone to the other extreme...making love right in their presence."

"Both approaches are wrong. But I'm the one who was supposed to be laying down the ground rules," she said.

"Maybe I should go home, so you can get through to Esko easier?" I suggested. She didn't respond, just looked at me intently. I got dressed and drove away from Emerson Woods in the dark and silent night.

CHAPTER TEN

1985 Shanni

During the unusually hot and humid summer, Mayu's anxiety about losing the house and her sporadic run-ins with Hannu were cumulatively having an oppressive effect on me. Mayu was moody and ready to find fault with everything I was or said or did. I was reaching the breaking point. I began to ask myself, why do I keep seeing this woman?

Mayu was quite candid about her domestic situation and didn't mince words. She often asked, "Why *do* you want me? Here I am with two boys, a dog, and all the negative emotional baggage of a divorced woman."

But there was something at work inside me. One warm night when we were taking a walk by the Emerson Woods pool, I had a spell of unusually fast breathing. I felt as if I couldn't catch my breath. It took me several minutes to return to normal and I didn't know what was going on. But Mayu peered at me penetratingly. This happened several times over a period of weeks. Finally, Mayu spoke to me as we were sitting in my car outside her house. We were just returning after an evening in Washington. "Why don't you put into words what your body is trying to say? If you verbalize your feelings, you will stop losing your breath and your body will stop doing these convulsive acts."

For a moment, I didn't respond to her. I wasn't sure what she thought my body was trying to say. She was encouraging me to voice my feelings, but I didn't really know what they were.

"You have fallen in love with me, and since you haven't chosen to say it to me, your body is saying it for you," she told me. "You know, divorced women are very wary of men...and are very reluctant to form new relationships. Their initial hurt prevents them from doing so. I remember you told me once that you thought you were incapable of loving, but you have come to love me in spite of yourself. I can't reciprocate, at least not now,

anyway. But I will be caring and considerate to you...and just."
When she finished, she pulled me toward her in a semi-embrace.

Why indeed should I love her? Why in God's name fall in love with a woman with so many encumbrances when there were so many women waiting to be appreciated? I asked myself. I could not come up with an answer. The more I asked, the more remote the answer became. All I knew was that if I didn't see her, I felt like I was going to die. Ever since I'd met her, other women ceased to exist for me. They were all around, they would come into view, but then seem like a movie out of focus. I knew Mayu's past, the poverty-stricken childhood and the womanizing husband, and I had often commiserated with her. Her overly aggressive behavior, I thought, is in self-defense and is her way of getting back at the world. I remember her telling me often, "When I was a teenager, my reality was the only reality, I thought." It was a reality of poverty, suffering, lack of acceptance, and sometimes of shame. Shame on account of her drunken father who had no qualms about his daughter seeing him in bed with a whore; shame on account of her husband who would not hesitate a moment in seducing other men's wives. She had been wronged by men. She had been wronged by the world.

And yet, when I remembered her words—"my reality was the only reality"—I realized to what a great extent that isolation was still a part of her consciousness. For Mayu, what she thought and what she felt *was* reality, and anyone who crossed her was automatically wrong. It was as if she had turned her childhood shame and isolation into a virtue, a fortified castle that no one could enter. When I saw to what extent the world had maimed her, cut her off from the flow of give and take in life, I was overwhelmed with pity for her situation. But it was not just her suffering that made her attractive to me. She had an unusual brilliance that she exuded through every pore of her body, through every gesture, through every comment. It was never boring being with her. But it was never easy, either. Shades of gray did not exist in her life. Things were right or wrong, beautiful or ugly, lovable or abominable—and that went for people, as well. When she liked somebody, she was so effusive in her praise that it was totally out of proportion to the object of her enthusiasm. If it happened to be a man, it was a safe bet that she had fallen in love with him. And if she did *not* like somebody, the object of her contempt might as well be guillotined. I always forgave her. Knowing her past, I felt that it was all I could do.

"Let me take you to Canada," I said to her one day. As she stared at my face vacantly, I added, "What with the issue of the house, the boys and the job, you've got to get bogged down eventually. Why don't we get away from it all for a while? I know if I see one more struggling student I'm going to go stark raving mad."

"Speaking of the job, how can I? Irja Winston wants Jukka and me to sit down, since we're not teaching now, and complete the exercises in the Finnish book we've been working on."

"Mrs. Winston has been working on that same book for the last ten years," I sniffed. "If she somehow managed without you during that time, she can certainly manage without you for five days."

A smile spread over Mayu's face, as she realized that the trip might indeed be possible. Then she assumed a serious demeanor. "Mrs. Winston received her Master's degree in teaching Finnish a quarter of a century ago and she was approaching this book with totally outmoded techniques until I arrived on the scene."

As Mayu warmed to the task of criticizing her supervisor, I felt a twinge of concern. "I hope you haven't been too blunt in pointing out Mrs. Winston's shortcomings?"

"What do you mean, 'too blunt?' I told her how I felt and made it clear what was not working. Jukka has been there six years and has never had the guts to say it to her face...even though he complains about her all the time behind her back."

I winced. "I think we have strayed too far from the subject. I was simply thinking that you need a vacation and so do I. Maybe we can take a few days off, combine it with the weekend, and drive up to the cool clime of Canada?"

"'The cool clime of Canada,'" she said, mocking the bucolic romanticism of my words.

I laughed. "I admit it," I said, "I'm an incurable romantic. A sunrise can move me to eloquence."

"Oh...is that what you call it?"

"Take me or leave me."

"I'll take you." She laughed. The realization of how tired she was and how badly she needed some time off seemed to hit her. Her entire body sagged. Wiping the sweat off her face, she surrendered. "Let's do it. I've gone to Finland every summer of my life, but it doesn't seem like I'm going this year. So if we don't go to Canada, I won't get any vacation at all."

****

Debbie, Robert's new wife, had particular difficulties with Hannu's recalcitrant attitude and she couldn't see her way clear to taking the two boys and a large dog—a creature of Nature rather than human training—into her house for five days. Her house seemed to be designed for a future world where there would be no children to spill pizza on the couches or leave sticky fingerprints on the refrigerator door. Debbie and Robert lived in the affluent wooded enclave of McLean, a fair distance from Emerson Woods, which, she pointed out, also meant that the boys would be cut off from their friends and familiar environment. When Mayu asked Robert point-blank if he would take the boys, he showed no inclination to make Mayu's Canadian vacation with her new boyfriend any easier. Finally, Debbie came up with a solution. "Leave the boys at their own house and we'll be in touch with them by phone and visit them every evening after work."

Since Debbie worked at the same office where Robert did, the American Insurance Association, it would be easy for them to drive down together. Mayu felt uneasy about leaving the boys in the house without an adult on the premises, however, she would have been even more uncomfortable with leaving them with their father and his wife. The boys—especially Hannu—had often complained to her after visits about how rigid and "stuck up" they were.

"Dad's completely changed now," Hannu said. "He's not the dad I used to know." There was bitterness in his voice. "I have to be a certain way," he complained. "I have to dress in a certain way and, if I don't, Dad gets really mad. One time, I wasn't paying attention and Dad yelled at me, 'In my house, you pray at the table before dinner.' When I looked at his wife, she was nodding to reinforce what he had said. Those two look like Siamese twins, I swear to God. I wanted to ask them if the God they were praying to believed in men sleeping with women who were not their wives, but I thought, what's the use? They wouldn't understand. They wouldn't even get the joke."

Debbie and Robert went to church every Sunday, Hannu told Mayu, and their entire social life revolved around the church. "I just hate organized religion and I don't want my children indoctrinated by it," Mayu said. As she spoke the words, her emotions flared up until her face had the angry confusion of Hannu's. Her anger waning, she said with amazement in her tone, "Hannu once said to me that his Dad was 'a dick.' It was so graphic, what he said, that I knew then just how visceral his hatred was for his father."

I asked, "How does Esko feel toward his dad?"

"Robert has always been very kind to Esko, so Esko feels very warm toward him. He doesn't understand Hannu's hatred. That may be one of the reasons the boys just don't get along so well. They can't agree on whether their dad is someone to love or hate."

By the time Mayu and I left for Canada, it was a day later than we had planned. Hannu was nowhere to be found to be given guidelines for his short spell of freedom, or even for us to say goodbye. After waiting for him for a reasonable amount of time, Mayu relied on a hurriedly scribbled note that she left on the cluttered kitchen table under the bright ceiling lamp. We finally pulled out of the driveway, laden with sleeping bags, a green army tent with mosquito netting, thermos bottles, and all the rest of our camping paraphernalia. Barefoot in the driveway, Esko was watching us load up and asked when we would be back. Gypsy's face briefly appeared at the window, then she pushed the door open and came bounding after the van, barking and protesting that she didn't want to be left behind.

Roads tend to transform people and highways do it with a vengeance. As we got on the Washington Beltway, I felt as if we were cut off from our previous lives and were headed for a new beginning. We drove west for a while, to join the highway that went north to the Canadian border. The day was just ending and it felt as if we were literally driving off into the sunset. Mayu put on sunscreen and sunglasses; her sensitive Finnish eyes were never able to endure the direct rays of the sun. She talked on into the dusk, accompanied by the drone of the faithful little VW engine, propelling us into the future. Faster cars whisked past us. Then, we lapsed into silence.

"Gosh, I'm hungry," she said, suddenly. No rest stop was in sight, but we kept looking, and finally exited into a small road that promised nothing but a small town. In the dark, the view didn't matter, so we pulled off to the roadside somewhere. It was raining. As I busied myself converting the rear of the van into a dining room by setting up the table, Mayu pulled out some Finnish rye bread, smoked turkey, a cucumber, tomatoes, scallions and cheese, and made sandwiches. Taking a healthy bite, she said, "Smoked turkey is one American food I like very much. It's too bad they don't have it in Finland. When I leave the United States, I'll miss it."

"You introduced me to it," I said, "and now I'm also hooked." I wasn't one for eating cold sandwiches for dinner, but the food tasted very good and I settled down across from Mayu with a cup of hot tea. The rain was falling rhythmically on the roof of the van like the beating of a pulse. We could no longer see outside; rain and darkness had created a barrier and we didn't know where we were—nor did we care.

The past no longer exists, the future may never come, so the present is the only reality, I thought. We cleared away the food, folded the table and pulled the bed out. Mayu watched me with amusement, as I sprinkled cologne on my side of the bed. But she made no comment on my scent fetish.

"We revolt against our parents and it's really interesting how that rebellion gets manifested," I mused.

"What do you mean?" she asked, puzzled. In the strong light of the battery lantern, the depth of her questioning was clear on her face.

"My father was a kind of hippie, long before anybody had coined the word, and that was in a most unlikely place…a princely state in India."

"Was he revolting against his own father?" she asked.

I was startled by the acuity of her perception. "Don't I have any secrets from you?" I asked.

"No," she said in a tone of affected boredom. "I can read you like a book. So…what about your father?"

"Oh yes, he certainly was revolting against his own father. My grandfather was a fastidious man who even had custom-made gold buttons inscribed with his name on his sherwani…his Indian longcoat. When he rode to court where he was a judge, a footman standing in the rear of the carriage would be shouting to alert pedestrians and send them scampering away."

"Where was this?" Mayu asked, fascinated. "I know India. Where in India?"

"Central India. Before independence, there used to be a princely state called Gwalior and he lived in Lashkar, the capital."

"Go on. Tell me about your family history. It sounds interesting."

The rain seemed to have subsided and silence reigned all around us. Lying next to a Finnish woman in a van, somewhere in the countryside in the United States, I was trying to think of my lineage, of my past. While a bond of feelings existed between me and Mayu, a gulf of culture also existed—of our different life experiences, of our different viewpoints. While I was wondering how best to convey my family history across the cultural lines, I was gripped by the sadness which had haunted me all my life when I thought of my family.

Memory is a funny thing. We think of memory as a sort of pale part of the mind that keeps the residue of what was once action. But when we strike a nerve and an image of a moment that was powerful for us comes into focus, feeling floods into the present moment with an urgency that is sometimes even more powerful than our present sense experience. I always felt that way when I thought of my father. I always blamed him for the downfall of our family. "So," I went on to tell Mayu, "my father didn't wear buttons, let alone gold buttons. He walked rather than use a carriage. I'm surprised that he even wore shoes. He took the family to a small town and tried to live the life of a poor villager. In the very dawn of my consciousness, I recognized what was happening and decided to wage an unremitting war against that lifestyle. I became Mr. Fastidious in response to his lackadaisical approach to personal hygiene, countered his shabby clothes with custom-tailored three-piece suits, and met his body odors head on with a battery of colognes. In essence, I became obsessed with order. And to top it all off, I left town at the first opportunity and headed west."

Mayu lay listening, not uttering a single word, not a sound. "My father used to say to me, 'Why be so ambitious? All a person needs is a hut for a house, a cot for furniture, two flat breads and vegetables for food, and a shirt and baggy pants for clothes.'

"My father and I could never agree on anything, except that we were very different. He didn't know how to be a father and it used to make me very sad. It troubled me to see how other fathers talked to their sons and gave them guidance, which he couldn't do for me. I am sorry that he died and we never made our peace." I began to sob. Mayu reached out and held my face against her body. She wiped my tears away. "But I've forgiven him now, I guess," I told her, straightening up, "having come to know that his mother died in childbirth and his own father remained distant, probably because of his young second wife and their two children. He could never learn to be a father, to be a model for a young boy who needed him. He was always so awkward...I don't know how I got into this subject," I said softly. "Let's just drop it."

"The subject of fathers is a touchy one for both of us," said Mayu, surprising me with the depth of her sympathy. "I guess we've both had enough for one night." After a long pause, punctuated only by the pattering rain, she continued, "But I feel like talking about my mother. She was the epitome of motherly virtue. She made so many sacrifices in raising me that I'm always measuring myself against her when I assess myself as a mother...and I'm always finding myself falling short. When she died, I didn't know how I could survive the pain. Her funeral was quite a sight. The pallbearers were her brothers and cousins from the country—ill-dressed men with large hands and lined faces.

"You complain about your family fortune coming down and claim to feel badly about it. That's the difference between us. I didn't feel ashamed of my country relations being side by side with my brother, who was several cuts above them. And right next to them were my children, who were growing up in very privileged conditions. Three generations of my family, side by side, with a world of difference between them. But when I looked at my poor country relations, I said to myself, that's where I came from and I don't want to forget that. I don't want my children to forget that, either. When my children are old enough, I want them to go to the village where my mother's people lived, and realize with pride that they are links in that chain. I doubt very much that you would have felt that way, if you had poor relatives living in the country. That is a fundamental difference in our personalities."

A light wind was blowing. I could hear it, as it tried to sigh through the seams around the windows. As it grew stronger, the wind rocked the tall, narrow van. Dawn was breaking and we raised our heads and looked outside, wiping away the mist that had clouded the glass pane. We were on the edge of a small farm; green stalks of corn were swaying as though moved, caressed, mesmerized by the wind. The whole waking world seemed so dream-like that, even now, when I think back on that night, I cannot remember when we finally fell asleep. It was as if we effortlessly slipped from outer dream into inner dream. We felt only the absolute peace of having nowhere to go.

****

"I never thought New York State could be so beautiful," Mayu exclaimed, with a mixture of astonishment and pleasure.

"With New York," I told her, "people always conjure up an image of Manhattan concrete and totally forget the lush greenery, the rolling hills and the placid lakes in the rest of the state." I was just as pleased as she was with the pastoral vista. The night before, the rain had bathed everything, making it clean and fragrant. At the wheel, I could only steal a look to the left or right, but Mayu stared out the window, entranced. We were somewhere in northern New

York on Highway 81. Every few miles, there was another sign announcing a large body of water. Without consulting Mayu, I exited and headed west.

"Where are we going?" asked the eternal questioner. Her mind was still on a different plane and didn't seem to be concerned with how or why—and the *where* was almost a reflex action—just so long as we continued on in the same state of pleasant stupor, with sunlight streaming through the windshield and the whole van vibrating. It was as if somebody had carefully excavated a piece of earth and gently filled the hollow with the cleanest water to be found on this earth. We were on the south shore of Lake Ontario. We walked carefully on the beach, trying not to disturb the clean, sparkling sand until we gently submerged ourselves into the calm water. Mayu said, "The temperature of the water is perfect." I tried to frolic, to be playful with her, but she swam, single-mindedly wrapped up in herself, her brow furrowed. She didn't seem to know that I was there, as she doggedly pursued her breaststroke. There was no wind and the water was so calm that you could see for miles on its surface just by raising your face above it. "This water is so warm, it feels like you're swimming in a giant bathtub," Mayu said, stopping her strokes. "I think that's enough for today."

Drenched and dripping, she emerged from the water, her short blonde hair sticking to the side of her face. Her swimming suit did nothing to camouflage the extra pounds that had dogged her from country to country. She sat down in the bare sand with a sigh. The bright red sun continued to descend toward the horizon. When I turned and looked at her, I was startled by the expression on her face. She looked stricken and there were tears in her eyes. I sat down and took her hand in mine. She began to talk, but not to me. As the words tumbled out of her mouth, it was as if she were talking to herself. "I miss my cabin. I had enjoyed selecting the spot for it so much...an island on Lake Saima...building it and then spending summers there. It was like my umbilical cord, my link to Finland, and now it's gone. I will never forgive Robert for forcing me to sell it." She stopped talking for a moment, as the tears flowed. I didn't say anything. There was really nothing that I could say. Instead, I put my arm around her. "I used to sit by the cabin and watch the lake for hours. Every year, I waited for summer and looked forward to going to my cabin. And now, I can't anymore."

"What happened to the cabin, Mayu?" I asked her.

"We sold it as part of the divorce settlement and Robert got the money. Now, I have no place to go for summers in Finland."

Thinking that the beautiful view of Lake Ontario was having the opposite effect from the one I had intended, I decided to remove her from the shore and take her to the more neutral environment of the parking lot where the van was parked. "Let's go and have something to eat," I said. There were no bathrooms in sight and she disappeared into the bushes. When she re-emerged, she was scratching herself.

"I have this awful itching," she complained.

"Maybe you brushed yourself against some poisonous plant or something in the water? Since we were swimming in the fresh water, it couldn't have been a man-of-war or a jellyfish," I told her, my arm around her shoulders. But her expression remained frozen. She shook her head and began to scratch herself even more vigorously. "You know what all the dermatologists say about scratching...you shouldn't." I tried not to sound like a scold, but I was worried about her. I unlocked the van and began to set up the stove. She didn't help me. Instead, she remained preoccupied with her itch. Standing barefoot on the sandy surface of the parking lot next to the van, she sipped her coffee, nibbled on her flatbread and began to retrieve her past.

"Two years ago, during the summer, Esko and I travelled from Sweden to Finland and went to Aini's cabin. On the boat from Stockholm to Turku, Renny had this mysterious disease and had been itching, but there was so much sexual tension between us that neither of us paid much attention. After the first night at the cabin, I began to itch and had these reddish blotches all over my skin. A day later, Esko was itching and he developed the exact same kind of blotches. Renny had brought a medicine from Sweden that had to be applied directly to the skin, followed by a bath...all the while washing all of the clothes, including the bedding. The presumption was that the problem was caused by tiny creatures penetrating the skin and that they could live on the clothes for a while. To get rid of them, you had to attack them on all fronts at the same time. So, we went through the ritual, stripped off all our clothes and applied the medicine. We washed all our clothes and bedding and everything. While we were cleaning ourselves in the sauna, we heard voices. It was Eero, Aini, Sami and Mari coming in. It was so embarrassing…the mattresses and the bedding things were lying outside on the grass all over the yard, the cabin was in a shambles and all three of us were crowded in the sauna. Since the Tervalas were just returning from abroad and I hadn't talked to them yet, they had no idea we would be there."

"Who's Renny?" I asked.

"Oh, you're jealous? Your face looks ashen. But, Shanni, it's in the past. Renny helped me through a very difficult time. When my marriage was breaking up, he helped me keep my sanity."

"How? Where did you meet him?"

"The night when my marriage had reached the absolute breaking point, I called my friend Elli and told her that I needed to come over right away and talk to her. When I arrived at her house, she said that she was on the phone—ironically enough, talking to Robert. She asked me to wait. It was 4:00 in the morning, the children were in bed and her husband Kaiia was in Zambia on a World Bank assignment. I was restless and fidgety, and Elli kept shushing me. When she wouldn't get off the phone and I couldn't bear the loneliness, I went down to the basement where Renny was sleeping and sat down on his bed. He was a Swedish guy, 27 years old, who was staying with the family while doing some renovation on their house. I had met him before and he knew about my marital problems. He only had a high school education; he was not the kind of man an educated person like me should have been attracted to. I touched him. He opened his eyes and didn't seem surprised. I told him what was happening. Since Elli had shut me out, I needed somebody, *anybody*, and he just happened to be there. He quickly understood my state of mind and began to hit me in a playful way. Then, he asked me, 'How do you feel now?'

"I did feel better. We ended up tumbling and wrestling on the floor, and then we made love. It felt so wonderful. I felt as if I were purged of all pain. That's how I met Renny."

Our journey resumed in silence, as the dusk dissolved slowly into night.

"I know how much it must hurt you when I talk about Renny," she said, putting her hand on mine. "But at a time when my self-esteem was gone and my self-confidence was at its lowest point, he helped me tremendously. We wound up traveling around together that summer and it was a life-saver. While Robert was telling me that I was sexually inept, Renny was saying that sex was great between us. He was really young and he had just atrocious taste in clothes. People used to stare at the two of us and I could see in their eyes that they were thinking, what's that middle-aged, middle-class woman doing with *him*? But I didn't care.

"He showed so much maturity, so much innate intelligence and sensitivity that I was really taken by him. Actually, I fell in love with him. And the fact that he had a wonderful relationship with my children, especially Esko, made it even easier. But then again, it's in the past. He's back in Sweden and I haven't heard from him in ages."

"Yes," I said, firmly, "it's in the past. And we should keep it there." I guess it was in the past, but I knew that Mayu was still feeling the pain in the present. I could occasionally see her face lit up by the headlights of the oncoming cars. It was a sad face, telling the tale of a spurned woman. The sight of her face moving in and out of sight had a greater impact on me than if I had seen her continuously. I floored the gas pedal and drove the van as fast as its little motor could propel it, thinking that the fast pace might somehow shorten the period of her suffering.

"How is the itching now?" I asked her, keeping my eyes on the road, as I sped along at 70 miles per hour.

"I forgot all about it," she said, with a start. "I guess I'm not itchy anymore."

"Good."

We crossed the Canadian border and headed north. We finally saw the sign for the campground with boating facilities on Rideau Lake that I had picked out as our destination for the night. It was past 11:00 o'clock and I wondered if we would be able to get into the campground. The lights were still on in the office. When I parked outside, Mayu looked at me as a little girl might look at her father and said, "I'll wait here, while you get us a camping space." I looked at her and couldn't tear my eyes away. "Although I act rough and aggressive," her body seemed to be telling me, "I like to be weak and protected. I feel very secure in your hands right now and whatever you do will be in my best interest." Is this the same woman, I wondered, who on many occasions has pushed herself to the fore and insisted that she wouldn't accept any help...that she had to deal with people herself?

When I walked into the office, there were two elderly ladies winding down a tête-à-tête. "We're closed, sir," one of them interrupted the conversation long enough to tell me. The other one looked on, smiling pleasantly.

"But, Ma'am, we've come all the way from Washington, D.C.," I said meekly, "and my companion is very tired."

The second lady looked at the manager appealingly.

"All right. If you have a self-contained vehicle, and it looks as though you do," she said, peering out the window at the van, "park it anywhere for the night. In the morning, my son will come and register you."

The following morning, we opened our eyes on the still blue waters of the lake. "Oh, there's an island in the middle of the lake," Mayu said rapturously, sitting up on the bed and looking out through a slit between the curtains. When we registered at the office, she asked the man behind the desk if we could go to that island.

"It's not forbidden," he said. "But I wouldn't advise it. It's overgrown with poison ivy." Mayu didn't respond, but scrunched her face into that defiant look I had come to know.

We had parked overnight by the marina, so when we moved to our allotted space within the designated camping area, the lake, as well as the island, disappeared from view. Mayu's defiant expression reappeared.

"Let's rent a boat and row to that island," she said.

An hour later, I was rowing. The wind was heavy, and at times I felt that the wind carried the same message for Mayu as the man in the office had given her. I felt exhausted from rowing and still, the island looked as distant as ever. I began to wonder if it was an illusion, a mirage. I didn't want to complain, as I was afraid she would tell me, "I've coped with heavier winds at Lake Saima. So what are you talking about?"

When we finally landed, I wondered whimsically whether I felt the same relief at reaching land that Columbus must have experienced. I looked at Mayu. She now had an expression of complete satisfaction on her face. It was not a virgin island. There was plenty of evidence that people had trodden the island before. Carrying the boat cushions, we skirted around the litter of bottles and rusted metal cans. Finally, we came to a spot on the other side of the island, where the ground was level, the vegetation untrampled and no litter was in sight. Side by side, we sat down on the cushions and looked out at the white waves. She was more happy and relaxed than I had ever seen her—now that she was far away from all the things that usually tried her patience. As she sat there, I was filled with tenderness for her, so absorbed in the beauty of the water.

"I like Canadians much more than I like Americans," she said. "I have come to love Canada in the short time that we have been here. It's so much like Finland, with the crispness of the air, the purity of the water and the unspoiled forests."

****

We camped out for two days, shorter than we would have wished, with little to do but rest and enjoy the scenery and each other. On the third, the day of our departure, we went swimming in the lake right after breakfast. I was taken aback that Mayu was being stiff, aloof and matter-of-fact. She could hardly keep her hands off of me before, but now she had not touched me since breakfast. Sensitive as I was to her most subtle shift of mood, I saw her distancing herself from me and my heart immediately became heavy. She talked a little, but her communication was stiff.

Headed back, on a very tiny lake surrounded by coniferous trees, we had our picnic lunch. Still, I received the same monosyllabic communication from her. I didn't want our moment spoiled. The place was beautiful and it reminded me, also, of Finland. We were leaving Canada, but I didn't want to leave such a beautiful country feeling so morose.

"What's the matter, Mayu?" I asked. I couldn't bear it any longer. But she was evasive. Back on the road again, I asked a gasoline station attendant how I could get on the highway back towards the U.S. border. I focused on the road, taking in the part of Canada that we were passing through, but I couldn't untangle my feelings about Mayu. Enveloped in her dark glasses, she was sitting not far from me on the passenger seat, but she was so inscrutable that she might as well have been in another country.

"You talked to me this morning as if I were a child. It upset me very much." She caught me off guard with this comment, as I was negotiating a change of lane. I didn't remember ever thinking of her as a child or addressing her as one. I found myself in the wrong with her so often and hurting her feelings, without ever meaning to.

"What do you mean?" I asked. She gave no response. An impenetrable curtain remained between us. "I'm sorry if I did that," I said. "I certainly didn't mean to." I touched her hand, as a peace offering. She didn't move for several moments and then slowly took my hand in hers and squeezed it.

After we crossed the St. Lawrence River and took the elevator up to the Thousand Islands observation tower, we looked down at the road spanning the river, where we had made our tenuous truce. "I always need to talk before I can resolve things in my mind," Mayu said, looking down.

****

When we finally arrived back in Virginia, Mayu was taken aback by the condition of her house. It appeared as if it had been hit by a cyclone. "What the bloody hell is going on in here?" she screamed, more to vent her feelings than to elicit an answer. She thought that the children might be with their father for the day, but Esko was home and came running up the stairs to greet his mother. He had a bag of potato chips in his hand.

"What happened here, little Esko?" she asked.

"I don't know. I was at Dad's for the weekend. Hannu didn't go. Didn't want to."

Mayu sat down at the kitchen table and pulled Esko onto her lap. He pretended to be embarrassed, but I could see he really enjoyed Mayu's affection. "Oh my God, you're getting big! It won't be long before I won't be able to hold you any more." Mayu squeezed him and, after showering him with kisses, turned back to me and said, "He's much bigger for his age than most kids are. Look at these beefy thighs. He's five years younger than his brother, but he's already wearing the clothes Hannu wore last year. Speaking of that little wretch, where the hell is he? Why does that boy give me so much grief? I never should've let him out of my sight."

Mayu brusquely pushed Esko off of her lap, without seeing the hurt look on his face. He headed down to the rec room again to resume his TV watching. Mayu walked out of the kitchen and I followed. Her first stop was the living room. As she stood in the middle of the room, she caught sight of something and screamed. The scream was so frightful that I thought she'd seen a human limb or a cadaver. It turned out to be empty beer cans. I took her hand and moved her toward the bedroom, but she resisted. "You don't need all these hassles right after your vacation," I said, soothingly. "Lie down, sweetheart, and savor the trip. You need to recuperate." I removed the covers from the bed.

"I'm not lying on that," she said, shrinking from the bed so I could see the two pairs of pink panties and the telltale spots on the sheet. "Looks like some heavy-duty sex has been going on here," she said.

"Mayu," I said, "you don't want to be a hypocrite. We just came back from Canada, where we made love in the van and then walked around stark naked on a secluded field. And now you're furious because you've found a couple of pairs of panties on your bed? Don't you think that sounds a little petty?"

"No. It's not petty, and it's not a double standard," Mayu replied, sounding her usual argumentative self. "We can't apply the rules of adults to kids in their middle teens."

"But we can certainly keep from jumping to conclusions."

She stared at me, then spat out, "'Jumping to conclusions?' Give me a break! Any fool can see what's been going on here."

I was about to answer when I heard the loud bang of the front screen door, followed by Hannu's familiar, "Hello!" Mayu moved with a start, but I restrained her. In a few seconds, Hannu was at the bedroom door.

"What the hell has been going on here?" Mayu exploded. "You've been partying, while I was gone…"

Hannu looked at me, looked back at Mayu and, stretching his lips into a Cheshire cat grin, said in a very calm and cool voice, "Oh, Mom, we've been rehearsing a school play."

"With panties off and beer cans in your hands?"

Hannu laughed. "Yes, believe it or not. The play called for a bedroom scene and some beer drinking. So, for realism, we bought the beer and used your bedroom. Props, you know. I really didn't think you would mind."

I looked at Mayu to see how she would react to this outrageous explanation. Amazingly, a smile spread across her face. Whether she believed him, or was simply delighted in spite of herself by his gall, I don't know. In either case, she forgot her anger and looked satisfied. As Hannu walked off with the smugness of a poker player who has just drawn a winning card, I thought to myself, that boy will go far in life!

CHAPTER ELEVEN

1987 Mayu

After dinner, Esko tore out of the house, shouting, "Bye, Mom!" over his shoulder to me, as the screen door slammed behind him. A few minutes later, as I was clearing the table, I looked through the kitchen window and saw him playing ball on the school field with his new set of friends.

Sony, a dark, wiry, Indian boy, was one of them. His grandmother, who had recently come to live in the States, was baffled to find New World values superimposed on old ones here. "If I eat a hamburger and my grandmother has already taken a bath in preparation for prayers, she won't touch me," he confided once. At first, we didn't understand what he meant. It turned out that his grandmother was an orthodox Hindu. Because she was a vegetarian, whenever Sony ate beef, he became untouchable—well, at least temporarily.

Esko had also struck up a friendship with Tach, a ruggedly handsome boy. His father was a military officer attached to the Pentagon, a real martinet who often forgot that Tach was not a junior officer and frequently admonished him for not saluting or immediately "carrying out orders." I once asked him what he wanted to do when he grew up. He grinned and said, "Return to civilian life!"

Then there was delicate-looking Jeff, whose mother ran her house with all the civilized ferocity of an Emily Post School of Etiquette. Jeff did not oblige. Instead of being a model student, he played hooky. Once, left on his own, he invited Esko to go over and join him in urinating in a huge, expensive Chinese urn, one of the two in the foyer by the front door. Livid, Mrs. Post grounded Jeff, and then—if you can believe this—showed up at my door to demand 15 dollars from Esko's allowance. "Economic punishment," she said, "will discourage future infractions of the rules." She was horrified that I thought the whole thing hilarious and laughed at her reaction. My sticking by Esko so infuriated her that she now took every possible opportunity to malign my negligible housekeeping abilities.

Lastly, there was Esko himself, bigger than the rest, a child of nature, who was successfully groping his way into adult life—more or less. I was glad that after long lonely months of sitting at home, he had found a group of friends, however outlandish. He's declaring his independence from me just the right amount, I thought. We'd always been so much alike and were very close over the years. There were no words to express how deeply I would be hurt if he ever distanced himself—emotionally or physically—from me.

There were shrieks and shouts, as Esko made off with the ball. I felt proud and pleased watching my boy. I turned away from the window, only to be faced by a messy kitchen. Right on the money, Mrs. Post! I thought, wryly. I figured I'd clean it up after the news. I glanced at the clock, which was always five minutes late, and realized that *World News Tonight* would be starting shortly. I went down to the cool rec room and switched the TV on. There was a soft crackle and the picture didn't come into focus for a good 20 seconds. "I'll have to get this looked at sometime," I sighed, as I sank into a large old easy chair.

The local news was winding up. The anchor-woman was sharing a pleasantry with her co-host and signing off. I lazily wondered whether she came home from the studio to a sink full of dirty dishes and a house full of dog hair. My mind skipped to the mound of clothes behind me in the laundry room—some needing to be washed, some mended, some ironed, but all needing attention. I pulled my body up out of the chair to get the ironing board. It was an effort and a reminder that those extra pounds had to go.

As I pulled out the metal legs of the ironing board, the telephone rang. I started up the stairs to answer when I was knocked off my feet by a brutally sharp pain in my side. Finally, what I had feared all this time had happened. All the symptoms were there. The telephone was still ringing. If only I could get the damn thing, I thought. I finally crawled upstairs and picked up the receiver.

"Mayu, are you all right?" Shanni was shouting into the phone. I could hardly muster the strength to say that I was having a gallstone attack. "I'll be right over," he said and hung up. My pain seemed to have brought time to a standstill, but Shanni arrived quickly. He took one look at me and announced, "I'm taking you to the emergency room. I'll take care of everything." He said that, knowing how anxious I was about money. Still, I resisted going to the hospital.

"The pain will go away," I said, emphatically. "Trust me, gallstones are a national affliction in Finland. My mother had them, so I know the symptoms very well." But I knew then and there that I couldn't go on evading surgery. I had known of the stones' existence for many years, but despite my usual realism, I guess I kept hoping that they would somehow magically disappear by themselves. "But I guess finally this time the stones will have to go the prosaic way...under the surgeon's knife," I told Shanni. I smiled at my own good humor. I was feeling better.

"I know what I can do," I said, suddenly inspired. "Have the surgery done in Finland." I did a quick calculation in my mind—even with the airfare, the total cost of the trip ought to come to less than it would cost me to get the procedure done here, with the surgeon's fee and the hospital stay and all. Shanni listened to me dubiously. It had not occurred to him that I could get the surgery done there much more cheaply than in the States. "And of course, I would like you to come with me, if you can," I added.

"Actually," he said, firmly, "I would insist on coming with you." He touched my side with his fingertips, in anticipation of the pain that the surgery would cause.

Because of my job uncertainty, my finances were rather precarious. Irja Winston had been grooming Jukka as her successor in the Finnish Department at the Institute. He was a person with whom I had had a few run-ins. With Mrs. Winston's retirement imminent, I was fairly certain that I was not going to have a long future at the Institute. The Bogota Project could not forever be my claim to respectability when I went out job hunting, and I wasn't sure what kind of references I was going to get from my present job. I needed to get this operation done with the least possible financial pain. And I did so want to see Finland again.

"I'll pay the travel expenses for both of us," Shanni said, sensing my concern. But, of course, I couldn't accept that.

"No," I told him. "It's enough that you're going to be there for me. Just buy your own ticket."

I phoned Aini, my long-time friend, now living in Turku, with the idea of a trip to Finland. She was enthusiastic, which took away some of my anxiety. By the time I talked to her again a few days later, she had all the information for me about the hospital and the name of a doctor who had agreed to do the surgery. He was going to charge 2000 marks, or about $500. Thanks to Finnish socialized medicine, the hospital stay would cost me nothing.

Shanni insisted that I call the Finnish doctor. When I finally got him on the line, he said with characteristic Finnish brusqueness, "I'm going on vacation. I'll be back on the third of August. Be here on the tenth." That's a Finnish man for you, I thought, staring at the receiver that was now sounding only its dial tone.

****

What with arranging for the boys and the dog, and working up until the very last minute, I was exhausted when we left for Dulles Airport. It helped that my good friend Marion came along to bid me farewell. It *didn't* help that my long-time friend, Elli, showed up late with the car. Lately, Elli and I had been going through a sort of falling-out. At one time, we used to talk morning, noon, and night, sharing the most mundane details of our lives with each other. Though we came from different classes in Finland—her father was a college president—we found common ground through our friendship. Sure, we had our differences. She'd been married at 18 to Kaiia, who'd gone on to get a Ph.D. in economics and land a cushy job at the World Bank. She was now a housewife. I was actually jealous of her lifestyle. She was a woman of leisure, while I worked my fingers to the bone so my sons and I could barely scrape by. That wasn't as much a problem between us, though, until one day, in a moment of weakness, she told me how she and Robert had once prayed in a church, holding hands. *Great,* I thought bleakly. From then on, everything about Elli changed in my eyes. But I had to give her high marks for her tenacity. Never once did she give up on our friendship—no matter how much I rejected her. She admired Shanni, too, and she was very kind to him. The sad thing was that, by then, I was so suspicious of her that even if her intentions were totally innocent—which they probably were—I could never again trust her around a man of mine. But since she'd offered to drive us to the airport, I accepted.

During the drive, conversation with my friend Marion about her present consulting job, her hunt for a man, and her break-up with John that had been on-going for five years, kept my thoughts away from my irritation with Elli and my anxiety about the impending operation. Once on the plane, I collapsed in my window seat and fell sideways into the arms of Shanni. The captain announced that the jet was taxiing for take-off. Our seats were in the bulkhead, with a space in front of us instead of other seats. Without this cover, I felt as though I were in bed in public, with the stewardesses marching up and down the aisle. Ostrich-like, I closed my eyes and retreated into my own reality.

"Don't you want to wake up?" Shanni whispered into my ear. "We're reaching Frankfurt."

Frankfurt Airport's terminal always gave me the feeling that the whole world was converging at a point, with droves of travelers from Asia, Africa, North America and Europe crossing each other's paths. When I saw an Indian grandmother struggling down the ramp with her grandchildren, I thought, a new era of European discovery by the people of the East has begun. Then I looked at Shanni, my own mystery man from the East, watching our baggage as I went to a duty-free shop to buy presents for our Finnish hosts.

I had known Shanni for years now, but at this moment, I realized just how little I really knew about this Asian man beside me. Through all the unraveling of thousands of emotional strands, he remained a very private person. He was a lover who liked to be with people at his own sweet will, a misanthrope who had bursts of love for humanity, a passionate person who often professed his inability to love. He remained an enigma, a challenge requiring all the energy I could summon. In the beginning, I dismissed him as a simplistic Asian. Elli used to say, "Oh, Mayu, you're mistaken about him. Take him more seriously." What made me take him for granted were his excessive attentions, his solicitude, his desire to please me no matter what. Elli observed on another occasion, "If he remained aloof and distant, you would've gone running after him." I suppose she was right. I had initially approached him with the racial superiority of a European who considered it her burden to guide the poor savage through the intricacies of civilized life. Now, I wondered who the civilized one really was.

Once again, we were in the air. A group of Swedes was engaged in animated conversation and serious drinking. I was wide awake, occasionally picking up the dialogue, since I knew Swedish. We were headed toward Stockholm. Shanni wanted to break the journey there to do some sightseeing. I had made reservations at a youth hostel situated on a boat downtown. Stockholm is built on water and it would've been picturesque. But just seeing Swedish people and hearing their language, and the captain's announcement that we were getting close to Sweden, started to have the same old effect on me: I felt small. The facts—that I had lived in Sweden for four years, that Finland was prospering now as an independent nation, and that I now lived in the States—didn't change the age-old feelings of inferiority I felt as a Finn toward Sweden. "Do we have to stop in Stockholm?" I asked, aware that I was almost whining.

"Not necessarily," came Shanni's puzzled response. But the plane followed its own plan, touching down at the Stockholm airport, and we joined the exodus of passengers to the terminal waiting room.

"Do you mind if I speak about the change of plans to the ground personnel in English?" I whispered. Shanni smiled with understanding. I approached a tall, Viking woman and explained our change of plans. Somehow she sensed that, although I spoke English, I ought to know Swedish—maybe it's my coloring? Anyway, we had a little psychic tug-of-war, she speaking in Swedish and I responding in English. The bottom line was that Shanni and I were shortly on a plane for Helsinki. I was so depressed by this little brush with what I took to be Swedish arrogance that I slept the entire way.

Finland has a wonderful effect on me. Though the Finnish landscape, which was coming into view, was not much different to a foreigner than the Swedish landscape we had just left behind, I could feel the blood coursing faster through my arteries. Carrying our suitcases as we stepped out of the terminal, I could easily have gone down on my knees and kissed the soil—but such histrionics are not part of my personality, no matter how I feel. The sun was nowhere to be seen. As a matter of fact, there was a touch of nip and drizzle in the air. It was quite a contrast to what we had left behind in Washington. I felt a sense of elation and energy, enough to propel me through the whole of Finland.

"It's good to be back in Finland," Shanni said. "Shall we get a cab?"

"No. We'll take the airport bus downtown and then take a tram."

A very civilized, uncrowded tram took us to Mannerheim Street where an old-fashioned creaking elevator took us to the sixth floor. When we knocked, the door immediately opened and the smiling face of my old friend Maili welcomed us. I was shocked to see how she had aged and how much weight she had put on since the last time I was in Helsinki just a few years before. I did the introductions. Shanni was charming to her, but I could detect that he felt disappointment in Maili. She immediately took to him, though, and as she served tea at the tiny table in the tiny, grimy closet of a room—which served as a dining room, bedroom and storage room—she talked to him animatedly about her long-cherished desire to visit India. Later, her 17-year-old daughter, Anna, arrived from school. Seeing that she felt very comfortable around Shanni, Maili said, "Why don't you take Shanni on a sight-seeing tour of Helsinki, Anna?"

When they left, Maili poured out her heart to me. It was not the Maili I had known during my college days at Jyvaskyla, or even the Maili I had kept in touch with over 20 years, but a woman who had ceased to live. She had become so dependent on her daughter that she was choking her, while the limited space in the apartment did not provide any respite. She existed only for her work, integrating children with mental retardation into the school system. Maili had been married to a brilliant physicist, but the marriage ended in divorce. Not long after, he'd had a complete nervous collapse and was now institutionalized. Years had gone by, but Maili could not disengage her emotions from him. To keep men at bay, she created a shield of obesity and filth around herself.

When Shanni returned, we retired to our bed, which was not much larger than a baby's crib. I whispered to Shanni that we couldn't make love—not only because Maili was so close, but because she was so lonely. As we lay still, the silence was pierced, ironically enough, by the sounds of lovemaking from the apartment next door. The woman especially was very vociferous at the last.

"It's interesting that people like Maili like to confide in you and feel catharsis through it," Shanni whispered to me.

I thought about what he had said. The truth, I thought, is probably that I need miserable, needy, downtrodden people so that I can feel good about myself. I suppose even saints are hypocrites, if they don't acknowledge that they need life's evil to play their role.

In the morning, skirting the kitchen's crusty pots and pans and trying not to breathe in too deeply the smell of moldy fruit and dead mice, we managed a simple breakfast. As we gathered our things, Maili said, "I hope the porno video from next door didn't disturb your sleep too much." Shanni and I looked at each other and almost laughed because we hadn't figured out that the erotic encounter we'd overheard had not been for real. "It goes on every night," complained Maili. "We're thinking of filing a complaint."

"We were so tired that we slept right through it," Shanni said. I kept thinking about the complaint Maili was threatening to make against the lonely man next door. Is he really all that different from Maili? She may not have sought the same outlet, but they were suffering from the same affliction.

****

"My God!" I said, as I stepped into the tram that was to take us to the bus terminal. "It's already Friday, and on Monday I have to report to the hospital in Turku for pre-surgery tests." We stood in the rear clutching the passenger handholds, our suitcases upright, braced against our legs. The other passengers, all Finns, eyed us curiously but politely. They probably thought us an odd couple. But then again, this was Helsinki with its foreign embassies and its relatively cosmopolitan sophistication. And so many Finnish women were fascinated with foreign men that people joked that Finland's largest export was its women.

There was a loud thud and a strong jolt. The tram had collided with the vehicle ahead in the steady drizzle that had wet the tracks. All the passengers were shaken. Shanni was thrown against the bar which had braced him and I was thrown against him, his body cushioning mine. As I recovered my balance, I saw him wince with pain. As soon as he saw me looking at him, he put on a smile and said, "It's really nothing. It's just that I was taken by surprise."

Another tram picked us up and took us the rest of the way downtown. "No, we don't have to buy tea from here," I told Shanni. "You can get all kinds of tea in Turku and I'm sure Aini will have good tea. Aini is a very meticulous woman," I told him, as our bus to Turku picked up speed. "We became friends at Lahden Yhteiskoulu, where we both went for eight years. Her mother was a cashier at the same bank where my mother was the charwoman, but in this case it didn't stop us from being friends. Our friendship has survived long separations and the distance of thousands of miles. Aini says it's *because* of the distance that our friendship has survived all these years."

Shanni looked at the clean, comfortable bus appreciatively. "I don't know why we don't have public transportation like this in the States. It seems that there is a correlation between an egalitarian society and a good public transportation system," he commented.

"Ours is an egalitarian society, all right," the woman sitting behind me said. "Our president walks to the barbershop and gets his haircut in turn, just like everybody else."

Her words struck a chord in me. I felt as if I had drunk this ideal—that no one should place himself above anyone else—with my mother's milk. On the other hand, Shanni could never get rid of his class-consciousness, which was indelibly imprinted on his psyche. "With this kind of serious gulf between us," I had often said to him, "it amazes me that we got together in the first place, or that we stay together." I don't know what his thoughts were on the matter—he never gave me a reply—but it certainly was a problem in my mind.

As I was immersed in this thought, I heard the woman tell Shanni, "Our tax structure is such that it prevents the accumulation of excessive wealth by individuals, while our social services protect people from extremes of poverty." I was delighted that Shanni was getting this education about Finnish society from someone other than me—perhaps, I thought, it will help him to know why I feel so strongly about a classless society. My mother used to say, "If I had to be poor, I'm glad I was born poor in Finland, where society protects me from the harshest aspects of poverty."

"I strongly feel," I said to Shanni and our fellow passengers, "that it is a person's inalienable right to receive education and medical care—whether they can pay or not. It's a commentary on Finnish society that I'm returning here for my operation."

All of a sudden, Shanni became very quiet, with his mouth clamped shut in a way that I had come to recognize. We had had variations on this discussion many times before; I often complained that I needed to carry expensive medical insurance that I couldn't afford to receive medical care in the States. I think that the crux of the matter was, though he would never admit it, Shanni didn't like to hear his adopted country criticized, even in the mildest way. At the beginning of our relationship, he used to say, "I love the United States because it has been a land of opportunity for me." But, in deference to me, he did stop singing the praises of the "land of the free" after he realized that I had seen no happy ending to my American Dream. I found that, as more and more years passed with me living in America, I seemed to feel more and more Finnish.

Time passed quickly, as we jounced along, chatting and watching the countryside pass by. It seemed that in no time at all we were at the Turku Bus Terminal. I could see the familiar face of Aini's husband, Eero, through the window. He didn't seem to have aged at all since I had seen him last several years ago. There wasn't a single new line on his face, his hairline was still where it had been, his stomach was still flat, and he seemed to be defying the onslaught of middle age. He seemed to be one of those people who would probably remain frozen in time, looking exactly the same whether in three years or 30 years. A young girl who must have been his daughter, Mari, was with him. But I would never have recognized her. Below the unfamiliar features of her long face, I could see the hallmarks of approaching womanhood on her lanky, girlish body. When she saw us, Mari shyly hid half-behind her father—hanging on his arm, as if that limb were somehow going to transmit to her a dose of social courage to deal with these strangers. Eero greeted us with a minimum of words. Ever taciturn, he had a surprisingly expressive vocabulary of gestures made with his large, capable hands. He transferred our suitcases from the bus to the trunk of his Volkswagen. "We're going to have lunch," he told me in Finnish, as he started the car.

"Where's Aini?" I asked. He told me she was at work. After that, I kept conversation to a minimum. Neither Eero nor Mari spoke English well enough to converse, and Shanni's Finnish was limited to a few basic words and phrases. I could never coax him to unravel the mysterious Finnish language. At the café where we got lunch, I served as interpreter and soon found myself working hard for my supper. Shanni managed to break through the shyness barrier of father and daughter, and the three were having a real conversation. It wasn't every day that Indians traveled to a distant Nordic country like Finland, and Eero and Mari were both proud of hosting this exotic visitor.

"When I get back to school, I'll have a great summer story to share with my classmates," Mari said. When the meal drew to a close, with a twinkle in her eye, Mari asked if Shanni had owned an elephant as a pet while growing up. We all laughed. Oblivious of the fact that Eero was talking about the lunch coupons he got from Finnish Broadcasting as part of his work benefits, Shanni tried to pay the bill which the waitress had dropped on the table. Eero stopped him.

"Let the Finnish workers extend their hospitality to you," I said, and Eero took it from there.

Not a thing was changed at Eero and Aini's house. We took off our shoes at the door, as we had always done. The only thing the house was missing was its mistress. She was still at work, as an executive secretary at the university. Eero and Aini's son, Sami, was away at camp. Eero informed us that it was in his room that we were going to stay while we were in Turku. In anticipation, they had removed the furniture and put down two long, narrow mattresses on the floor, covered with sheets, blankets and pillows. There was just enough room left to put down our two suitcases. We couldn't move about very well in the room, but we didn't have to. I was going to spend most of my time horizontal and Shanni was going to nurse me. Without a word, Mari disappeared into her room down the hall and Eero went upstairs, saying that we should yell if we needed anything.

"This is the house of a blue-collar worker in Finland?" Shanni said, as he closed the door.

"Did you notice that this is one of four identical houses? Four working-class families got together and gave the specifications to the builders. Now, they have joint heating and cooling, and share in the outside maintenance."

As we were talking, our hostess arrived home. She and I met as if we had been separated only a few hours instead of several years. I said, "Aini Tervala, meet Shanni Ali."

Aini was her usual self—small, meticulous, bubbly, making generous use of her arms and hands. During the quarter century that I had known her, like her husband, she didn't appear to have changed at all. It was interesting to see how she had maintained such girlish enthusiasm about life.

We all congregated in the kitchen. Aini was in the cooking area, moving fast on her small feet—talking rapidly and gesticulating with her hands, making preparations for dinner. I was looking forward to it. Food always tasted better to me in Finland's clean, crisp air.

On the other side of the counter from Aini, Eero sat within the little kitchen area on a tall stool. Mari was present but largely kept to herself. I was feeling right at home in a Finnish house, speaking Finnish, with familiar Finnish kitchen appliances clattering in the background. I admired the fact that Shanni didn't seem to feel left out. If he wanted to say something, he would say it unabashedly; if he wanted to address somebody, he would address that person, looking him right in the eye. Despite the language and cultural barriers, it was remarkable to see how quickly he became assimilated in a Finnish home. I didn't do much translating for him, since most of what we were talking about he already knew—the soap opera of my life with Robert, Hannu and Esko. I figured he could do without the reruns.

Aini asked me, "If your life hasn't worked out in the U.S., would you consider coming back to Finland?"

"How can I?" I asked. "According to my divorce agreement with Robert, I have to keep the boys within a radius of 250 miles of where he lives. And right now, he lives in the Washington area. So I can't do anything like that for at least another few years...until Esko turns 18."

When we sat down at the dining-room table, I felt an ache of jealousy. No, even envy wouldn't be too strong a word. At the same time, I felt ashamed of myself for this emotion. I liked Aini too much to want to feel this way toward her for her seemingly picture-perfect life, spread out before me like a tapestry.

I thought back on Aini and all we had shared over the years. Aini's parents' marriage was no more a success than my own parents' had been. In a moment of passion, her mother had married a much younger man, a sort of hippie from the era long before the term came into use. Somewhere along the line, as Aini's mother would say, "He'd just melted away." Yet, during their brief summer of marriage, Aini's mother had experienced no cruelty, no violence, no drunkenness, and no poverty—all the hallmarks of my mother's married life.

When we were girls, Aini's mother would sit on a chair, dressed in pretty clothes, dealing with people and money. It was the same bank where my mother, in her shabby clothes, was on her feet all day long, sweating either in the kitchen or behind the vacuum cleaner, dealing with dirt, garbage and leftovers. As if that were not enough, my mother had to cope with the moods of an alcoholic husband who claimed to have a stone for a heart. Aini's mother had family money, which was now all coming Aini's way. Continuing her streak of good luck, Aini found a husband for whom family, home, love, caring and fidelity were of paramount importance...not that she didn't complain about him.

"Eero is too sedate, too remote, too much of a homebody," she had often told me. "After work, he has no outside interests. He tries to satisfy his social needs at home. He's home every evening—Friday, Saturday, or any weekday—tinkering with tools, fixing things, or glued to the television. Meanwhile, I wait—day after day, month after month, even year after year—but he displays no affection. I long to hear him say, 'I love you.' Well, if one of these days the proverbial white knight shows up on his horse, I'm going to ride off with him." Although she used a jocular tone, I wasn't amused. I actually felt a wry sadness at the irony of life. All my life, I had wanted somebody like faithful, solid Eero. Instead, I ended up with Robert, who was everything I didn't want in a husband. *Lucky me!* I chose a husband, a man sophisticated and educated, but abusive in a thousand subtle ways.

Maybe I should say it was fate that had thrust Robert on me, as if I were doomed to recreate my previous experience. I still couldn't get over how the passion that we felt for each other in the early days had become such a deep freeze. According to what he reported to me, he'd told his psychiatrist that he couldn't have sex with me because he couldn't feel superior to me. No wonder he bounced from me to Debbie, with her high school education and her adoring cow-eyes.

I was sure that Robert and I were alike in the early days of our courtship and marriage, but as mask after mask fell away, I felt the cold chill of being in the presence of a total stranger. After we were married just a few years, during which he'd seemed to cherish the same values that I had, I suddenly found him critical as he unfolded beliefs that I never knew he had. His clothing became suspiciously Republican; three-piece suits, even a bow tie now and again. And, worst of all for me, he became a social churchgoer. Don't get me wrong, I have nothing but respect for sincerely religious people, but Robert used church to make himself look good. It was sort of like joining the right men's club, or getting a child into the right school. Anyway, the contrast between Aini's life and mine, and the way that fate had smiled upon her and frowned upon me, seemed stark indeed. Of course, I couldn't choose my parents, but I also couldn't exonerate myself from what happened later in my life. Aini created this life of hers, the kind of person she was, using her own mental blueprint and shaping her microcosm. In the space around her, everything bespoke taste, finesse and, above all, order.

As we sat around and my thoughts wandered away, moving in and out of the present, I had a feeling that harmony, happiness, and well-being surrounded Aini, who sat at the head of the dining-room table, presiding graciously at the dinner she had so carefully prepared and was now making sure was a success. Eero sat to her left, I to her right, Shanni next to me, and Mari next to her father, facing Shanni. As Aini meticulously carved pieces of the beautiful salmon she had baked in paper—which I'd never been able to find in the States—I couldn't help saying that, in spite of our being so different and being so far apart for so long, it meant a lot to me that our friendship had survived. When the dinner ended and we went down to the immaculate rec room to watch television, I was convinced that I couldn't have created a world like that for myself. Sitting next to Shanni, I wondered what kind of life was in store for me with him.

CHAPTER TWELVE

1987 Mayu

The big moment for which I was in Turku was drawing near. I thought there could be no better way to while away the time waiting for the surgery than going shopping. Most pressing was the matter of finding books for the Saturday Finnish language class I was coordinating back in Washington for the Presbyterian Church. I walked down the street with Shanni and we caught the bus for the market downtown. The square was bustling with produce stalls and farmers were doing a brisk trade, hawking their wares. Fresh strawberries and raspberries, lusciously ripe and red, looked very tempting. But they were expensive. Good food always seemed out of my price range in Finland. So I moved on to do the business that needed to be done right away—ordering the books and arranging to have them mailed to the States. Stockmann's Department Store will be the place to go, I thought, and I was right.

Everything moved smoothly until the matter of accepting a personal check drawn on a U.S. bank came up. Shanni looked at men's clothing, as I wrestled with this problem at the Customer Service window. When I finally joined Shanni, several hours had elapsed. But he didn't complain. I was amazed at the variety and quality of clothes for boys. But again, the prices were high. "There must be a lot of money in Finland," I said, as I went from display to display, imagining how different combinations of shirts, slacks and sweaters would look on my boys. Whoever had designed the displays had a flair for the dramatic—especially in the color schemes. It was a pity that the prices were just as dramatic. I did buy two shirts and a tie, then I high-tailed it out of there before I could buy another thing.

When we returned to the bus stop at the marketplace to catch our bus back to Aini's, the farmers in the square were in the process of dismantling their stalls. A few were still selling, but the pick of the fruit and vegetables had already been taken and I didn't feel like buying other people's discards.

This was the weekend I was supposed to prepare myself emotionally and physically to check into the hospital for processing and pre-surgical testing. My nerves were already on edge, and when I saw that something had changed Shanni's mood—he was locked inside his shell, non-communicative—I blew up. "What's going on?" I confronted him in a corner of the little balcony where he had retreated to write.

"Nothing," was his reply. And then the jerk had the gall to not even raise his eyes. Immediately, this kind of behavior—denying what was right before my eyes—triggered memories of Robert. It made me even more furious. But I did the best I could to check myself.

Modulating my tone, I said, "Don't insult my intelligence. You're not yourself and I want to know what the hell is going on."

"Listen...I'm doing everything I'm supposed to do...sharing the housework, looking after you. And now I'm sitting here in seclusion, not saying anything to anybody or bothering anybody, and you come here and start badgering me," he said. This was definitely my clue to leave him alone, which I did. I was convinced, however, more than before, that there was something wrong. All weekend, his behavior was correct. He was always good at that. He engaged in repartee with Aini, Eero and Mari, and even smiled at the appropriate moments. But the tension between us lasted all through the weekend. I could never understand people who bottled up their feelings. I don't believe in it. And furthermore, I seem to be incapable of it. Even if my mouth is shut, my feelings always come screaming out of my every pore.

****

When I opened my eyes after the surgery, they rested on Shanni's smiling face. He was sitting by my hospital bed, holding my hand. "I was so anxious that I couldn't concentrate on my writing, so I cleaned house. I was relieved when Aini called me and said that she had finally gotten hold of the surgeon. He told her that the operation had gone very well and that he had taken out the gallstones—all ten of them. The nurses said I could come visit you at 5:00, so here I am." He gently squeezed my hand and then kissed it. I felt absolutely no pain from the surgery—no doubt because of the painkiller my doctor had given me. But there was a nagging feeling from the I.V. needle. Shanni took a bottle of hand lotion out of the night table drawer and began to rub my legs and feet. It felt wonderful, as though all of my dark anxieties were dissolving into air and light. But I was so groggy that I couldn't keep my eyes open to enjoy the pleasure. Slowly, I slipped into a peaceful sleep.

When I finally awoke, I felt well rested but I could feel the stitches. Obviously, the effect of the anesthesia was wearing off. Shanni had never stopped rubbing my feet, or so he claimed. I looked around the large hospital ward. There were seven other Finnish women there, and most of them were looking with great curiosity and interest at this foreign man and what he was doing. I could almost read the thoughts in their eyes—why aren't Finnish men so expressive, so attentive to their women? Maybe that is why they lose them to foreign men?

When Shanni was gone, they all ooh-ed and aah-ed over the beautiful roses he had brought me. Roses are a bit old-fashioned for my taste, but they were all Shanni could find in the hospital florist shop. Although the women were obviously burning with curiosity to question me about him, they were too polite to do so without being invited.

It was a motley group of women, middle-aged, old, and very old. Hospitals are not the place you see youth, as a rule. It was interesting to see how each was different from the other. The middle-aged, obese woman in the far corner, opposite me, was all wrapped up in herself and constantly complained—whether there were listeners or not. On the other hand, the very thin 90-year old woman in the next bed showed a great deal of alertness and interest in the world around her, despite the fact that she could no longer walk. It was interesting to see her reading the newspaper, as she was wheeled around in her wheelchair by the nurses. She and I seemed to have similar views on political matters. She told me that I had done the right thing by getting the surgery done as soon as possible. If I had waited, the doctors might have had to take out a stone the size of an egg, as they had from her, which was both painful and embarrassing. Surrounded by all these women and hearing about slices of their lives, I felt I was both a performer and spectator on this stage where the theater of the real was being enacted. Amidst all of it, I forgot my pain.

When Aini and Eero came to see me, Aini said, "We're really glad to have your friend at our house. You're so lucky to have found a man like him." Aini could speak English after a fashion, so she had had an opportunity to get to know Shanni, while I was hospitalized. He had quickly learned the household routine and taken it upon himself to perform certain chores.

I told them how I had carried over some elements of my relationship with Robert to Shanni, and how that tended to sabotage what we had between us. Eero had to leave in a short while. "It's just as well," Aini said, sitting down. "It's not easy to talk to him beyond a certain level. It would be terrible if you lost Shanni, Mayu."

"I think that's exactly what I have been trying to do through all my actions...trying to lose him. I have been hurtful, I have been critical, and often I have been totally insensitive to him."

"Why?" Aini asked, almost in a whisper. We had been talking softly, so we wouldn't be overheard.

"You've known me since I was twelve and you've known my relationships with my father, my brother, and Robert. When a man begins to give me his unqualified and unreserved love, my whole system goes out of whack and I don't know what to do with it."

"What you're saying, Mayu, is that you question your right to be loved."

"Oh, absolutely. That's what I've been saying in this relationship without realizing it."

"So, the theme of your life," she said, "is that men don't love you, or if they seem to, then they must be lying. So you will go all out to destroy the love, saying in effect, you men are transplanting something into my organism which my body rejects."

After Aini left, I was steeped in my thoughts of what we had been discussing. I was surprised by a visit from my brother, Heikki, and his common-law wife, Aili. (He had been divorced from Sinikka for years now.) He and Aili had driven down from Lahti. It took me a while to adjust to the reality of their visit, but not long to confirm the source of my problem. Even a perceptive observer would not have suspected that my visitor was my brother. He walked in, immaculately dressed, followed by his tall wife, twelve years his junior, and inquired about the operation and how I felt. The only vaguely personal thing he said was, "It must be awful to be going through all this alone in a strange city."

"No," I told him, "I have a new man in my life now and he has come with me from the States and is looking after me."

From then on, for two solid hours, he talked politics at me as his wife listened meekly without so much as a word. A listener might have thought he was visiting a colleague from the union office. When he left, my head was full of Finnish politics, but my heart was sad and empty, as it always was after I saw my brother.

****

Shanni took me out on my usual walk. This time, we ventured farther afield. Soon, I would be discharged from the hospital. The wound had been healing very well and it wouldn't be long before the stitches could be removed. I didn't like the prospect of having a permanent scar on my stomach, but I didn't have much choice in the matter. How Shanni would react to it in our intimate moments I would have to wait and find out.

"What was the matter? What was wrong over the weekend?" I asked him.

This time, he didn't engage in evasive tactics. He came right out with it. "I wasn't bothered, actually I was delighted, that you were looking at clothes for the boys at the store there. But you didn't even take a moment to think what I would look good in, or to think about what I might need—even though I had flown all the way from the U.S. to be with you here and we are spending so much time together. I'm feeling taken for granted."

****

Three days later, I was convalescing at Aini's after my discharge from the hospital. Shanni had taken off for a two-day trip to Stockholm to do the sightseeing that my abrupt change in plans on the way to Finland had prevented.

"I wonder if the maternal side of me is stronger than the lover or the wife?" I confided to Aini, as we sat down and tried to catch up on our conversation.

"You know, Mayu," she told me, "you had such a devoted mother. She clearly left you a standard of motherhood that you find hard to live up to. The male role model you had, I'm afraid, will always be ineffectual or negative in your mind...as it will perhaps be in mine, too. You will always expect the worst from men, inadvertently giving signals to that effect, and like a self-fulfilling prophecy, the worst will come true." I wondered if that was what I had done to Robert; what I had been doing all my life—and what I was doing to Shanni.

When Shanni returned, I asked him to lock the door of the little room where we were spending our last moments. Though the stitches had been removed, I asked him not to look at the scar when he made love to me. It hurt a little, but I knew he had gone without sex for many days. He thought I wanted him, so he got excited, but was very restrained and gentle, resting his weight on his arms and legs. I felt a great relief that I had taken care of this. A great burden was lifted from my chest.

Before we said good-bye to my long-time friend and her family who had been so gracious, I asked Shanni to go shopping with me. I bought yarn, needles, and a beautiful pattern and began to knit a sweater for him. If Shanni noticed my sudden show of solicitude, he didn't make any comment on it, which suited me fine. I wanted to make up for lost time with as little drama as possible.

****

Shanni and I were buying some vegetables from a market stall for lunch when I saw my brother passing by. Obviously, he had not seen us, and as I watched him, I gathered courage to call after him. I felt pangs of shame. I had been in Lahti two days, staying with his ex-wife Sinikka, my old friend, but I hadn't called him.

"Heikki!" In spite of myself, his name left my mouth. Soon, we were sitting in a café, our bags of vegetables on the floor by our feet. Heikki showed no surprise at running into us like this—even though the last he had seen of me was in the hospital. Heikki knew very little English, so we talked in Finnish.

When we returned to Sinikka's apartment, where we were staying in her son Tommy's room, Sinikka listened with interest to our chance encounter with her ex-husband. Sinikka was home from the store where she worked, and Rauno, her boyfriend, came over and cooked for us. After the meal, we all sat down in the living room to watch television and I worked on Shanni's sweater. In spite of her 50 years, Sinikka still looked beautiful and youthful, and I could see Rauno doted on her.

The following day, Rauno took us in his old, ramshackle car on a sightseeing tour. First, at my request, we went to see the tiny apartment where I grew up. Actually, I wanted to show it to Shanni since he was writing about me. Memories of my childhood, some sweet and some bitter, came to the surface. Our next step was Lahden Yhteiskoulu, the scene of my many academic triumphs and social humiliations. Finally, I asked Rauno and Sinikka to drop us off at my brother's house. I could see it was painful for Sinikka, since she and my brother had worked together on the house and being there stirred many memories in her. Aili opened the door and took us to the living room, where Heikki was watching a soccer match. After giving us a curt welcome, my brother continued watching television. It was a strange visit and I was relieved when we left.

That night, when we returned to Sinikka's apartment, I felt awful. It was as if all of my old wounds had been opened up. I was glad for the presence of Sinikka and Shanni, who helped me through it.

****

When it was time for us to leave Lahti, we had one more stop on my sentimental journey. I wanted to go to my cabin on Lake Saima—or at least the cabin that had been mine. When our train stopped at Lapeenranta, I discovered my heart beating faster. There was so much of my life associated with this town. This is where Robert and I had come, seeking to fulfill my lifelong desire to have a cabin on a lake, and where, in the lumberyards and shops, we had collected the pieces of the dream. I had never thought that I would be coming here with a man other than Robert. I felt pain, a deep sense of loss, as I dialed the phone. The place where I had come every summer from the States, my little piece of Finland, was gone.

Tapio Kirjavainen, the man who had built the cabin next to ours, answered the phone and said he would be right over to pick us up. As he drove us to his house in town, he explained to us how every morning, he got up at 5:00 a.m. and drove to the Soviet border. From there, a bus took him to his workplace inside the Soviet Union where his company had a construction contract. His wife, Pirjio, cooked us supper. Their son, Antti, who was almost Hannu's age, took to Shanni and invited him into his room. There, he showed him all the posters of rock stars that he had collected.

The Kirjavainens gave up their big bed for us. Before retiring for the night, Tapio said, "The weekend is coming up. I'll take you to our cabin tomorrow and Pirjio will join us after she finishes work."

Tapio came home from work early the next afternoon. "That's the beauty of Finnish summers—it stays light until late into the evening," he said, as he loaded his things and ours into the trunk of the car. I felt grateful that we would have long daylight hours in which to see the cabin. We went down to the water's edge and got into the boat which Tapio kept docked at the pier. With every thrust of the motor, the boat leaped over the waves and my heart pounded faster and faster. We skirted the island of Suur-Jankasalo where the cabins were, whizzing by the conifers that seemed to have gathered at the edge of the water to welcome us.

"Soon we'll be there," I said, stepping out of the boat. We had hardly put our things down in Tapio and Pirjio's little cabin when the Kukkonens, who had bought my cabin next door, showed up with an invitation for dinner. I was very anxious to see my cabin again. The thought that somebody else owned it now brought flashes of the days when I was building it right along with the workers—piece by piece, beam by beam. When the cabin was completed, it proved to be the fulfillment of my fondest dreams. It was my Camelot, my paradise. Summer after summer, I went there, with Robert or without, but always with the boys. There were summers when we came here, and oblivious of the world, passed weeks in perfect tranquility.

Heta Kukkonen welcomed us effusively and we sat down on the porch holding our drinks. There was still some natural light left, though Heta had hung lights and candles both outside and inside, creating the effect of a conflagration. Amidst the din of Heta's non-stop chatter and her husband Eliel's mostly monosyllabic utterances, I imagined I could hear the voices of my boys splashing lake water on each other. It was so clear in my memory! Stolid Esko would sit in the boat, silent and patient, holding the fishing rod meticulously as if the way he held it, rather than the chance passing of a hungry fish, would assure a bite. Sly, wiry Hannu would stealthily swim up from behind and surprise his brother with a splash of cold water on the back of his neck. Esko would fly into a rage because his little fish had been scared away by his big brother, and scream and call for assistance from me. I remembered once when this same scene was unfolding exactly like this, but Esko really did have a bite, the two brothers ended up joining forces in reeling in the big fish. Screams of complaint turned into excited exclamations, as Robert and I, sitting right here, roared with laughter. The four of us ate that delicious fish for dinner that night. None of us had much expertise in cleaning fish, so we all had to pick a few bones from between our teeth, but no one seemed to mind. After the children went to bed, Robert and I made love and fell asleep naked in each other's arms, thinking that there could be no paradise better than this one.

"May I bring you another drink?" Eliel's pleasant voice jolted me out of my reveries and scenes from my lost paradise. His kind eyes were focused on me. I stole another look toward the lake. There were no children and the shouts of joy had changed into the sound of water lapping against the rocks on the shore. I accepted another drink from him and Heta suggested we all move inside. A pall of darkness was falling over the lake and it was just as well. Heta had the small table completely covered with dishes that she had prepared. The candles on the table burned at half-flame, seeming to reflect my feelings. I'm sure that Shanni was aware of how I felt, but he had his social mask on. He was very good at that.

I felt very strange occupying this cabin. It was as if my child had been taken away from me by force and given to the Kukkonens to raise. What is more, I didn't like the way Heta had decorated the cabin. Heta's taste superimposed on my cabin intensified my sense of paradise lost. I don't really know what I ate, drank, or said that evening because more vivid than the present was the film of the past—from the day we'd bought the plot to the day I got the news that it had been sold to the Kukkonens.

Back in Tapio's cabin, lying on the bed, I realized that a wonderful thing had happened; that I had been cured of my longing for my cabin. Hannu, my flamboyant son, so silver-tongued, had said to me on the eve of my departure for Finland, "Mom, you believe me, don't you? When I'm rich, I'll buy back our cabin." I suddenly realized that I had spent too much time shedding tears over this cabin. I had seen it again and it was not my cabin anymore and I would not want it to be mine ever again. There were too many bittersweet memories, and now this atrocious transformation.

****

Heta cried aloud, as we pulled away from the dock. I thought, I should come and visit these people—honest and sincere Finns who had gone out of their way to extend their hospitality to me, to us. But at the same time, I doubted that it would ever happen. There were too many memories and I wanted them to dim, even if they could never die. Mercifully, the boat's motor was powerful and the cabin, which once belonged to me and my little family, quickly receded from view. Nothing but the island and its trees and its eternity were left, as Eliel piloted us back to the mainland in the drizzle. Lake Saima had been there for thousands of years, since the glaciers formed it, and would be there for thousands more, but my own return was far more doubtful.

****

We returned to Helsinki, from where we would shortly fly home. As we waited for Heikki to pick us up at the train station, in the distance, I saw a foreign-looking man. He was tall, good-looking and in his mid-30's. Because he was looking around with the bewildered eyes of a man who was lost, I called out to him, "Can I help?"

He turned around, and began to bore into my body with his penetrating gaze. "Are you Finnish?" he asked.

"Yes."

"How come you speak English so well?"

"I live in the States. This is my friend Shanni."

He made absolutely no gesture to acknowledge Shanni and, at that point, it became clear that he had other intentions. "Will you help me look for an apartment?"

I didn't respond. Instead, I walked off as casually as possible, wishing him a pleasant stay in Finland.

Shanni was furious. He looked at me and said, "Don't you ever talk to strangers again."

"But I do and I will—especially to foreigners who seem to be in need of help in Finland."

"He wasn't looking for the usual help, you fool. That was clear to me when he looked right through me as if I wasn't even there."

"Do I look as though I have *stupid* written all over my face? Of course I figured out what he was after. But whatever he was going to get out of me is my affair..."

Shanni didn't pursue the debate any further, but I could see that his face was still distorted. The funny thing was that although the stranger was good-looking, I had no interest in him whatever. I found Shanni's jealousy comical. I like helping people in general, especially those who are visiting my dear Finland. It makes me feel good about myself and my country. What I don't like is being told what to do—by Shanni or anyone else.

A dark brown Honda with my brother at the wheel came into view. His appearance changed the tenor of our conversation. "I'll drive you to my son Sami's place," he announced, as we got into the car. "I called him and told him to get his vacuum cleaner out and use it," Heikki said with his characteristic brusqueness. "Mayu's guest has come all the way from India."

When we arrived at Sami's apartment, Sami had done what his father had asked him, a rare occurrence, since father and son had not gotten along since Heikki had abandoned him as a youngster. Sami had always been my favorite nephew—I could never understand his younger brother Tommy. Now, Sami had grown to be a tall, handsome young man of 25. He welcomed us with a warm smile. After proudly showing us around his little apartment where he lived with his girlfriend and their brand-new baby, who were not home, he went into the kitchen to prepare coffee for us. While Sami was busy putting together the refreshments, Shanni, Heikki and I sat down at the small kitchen table.

"It's now or never," Shanni proclaimed in the authoritarian tone which he had often assumed until I started to object. He trained his penetrating brown eyes first on me, then on Heikki and back on me again. He added, "You had better start interpreting this fast for your brother." I could tell from his face that he meant business and I began to interpret, as my brother looked toward him with a startled expression. "Mayu has shed so many tears on your account that you could easily drown in them. How come you're so hard on her when you know she's your only sister and that she loves you very much?"

"I don't know what you mean…"

"When your mother died, I'm told, you said on the eve of Mayu's departure to America that she was probably going to come back next time when you, yourself, died. During our recent visit to your house, you continued to watch television and totally ignored her, which made her absolutely miserable. But I know you love her very much. When you saw that I loved and cared for her, there was an expression of satisfaction on your face. So, why don't you express your love to her…in words and actions?"

My voice cracked, as I repeated this question to Heikki in Finnish. He looked very intently at my face. Then he spoke like a man who has been in pain for a long time. "Mayu received a top-flight education at the expense of the Finnish taxpayers and then went away to America to benefit that society, not ours. That's one bone of contention between us. Another is her putting on airs. She thinks she knows it all and her opinions are better than anybody else's. I can't take that crap from a kid sister, so I use devices to keep her in her place. Sometimes, she gives me the feeling that she's forgotten her working-class roots, and that makes me even more furious. As for my feelings for her, you're very perceptive: I do love her and care what happens to her. But I've never been a demonstrative person and I can't begin to be one now. Perhaps it's the legacy I inherited from my father?"

Heikki became quiet, as though startled at how long he had talked. Complete stillness followed his statement. The sharp whistle from the tea-kettle on the stove reminded us of where we were. And then something extraordinary happened—my brother got up from his place and embraced me. There were tears in the eyes of all three of us, as Sami came in from the kitchen holding the tray.

"Hold it!" he said, hastily putting down the tray. "Let me get my camera and record this moment!" My brother went back to Lahti, but not before he made the promise, of his own volition, to come and visit me in the States.

****

On the last day of our stay in Finland, waiting in Helsinki for our trip back to America, Shanni said, "I would like to buy a coat for you…a present, in honor of your successful recovery from the operation." We went downtown and went from store to store, looking for my coat. Finally, on the waterfront—ironically enough, in the very store where I had purchased the suit in which I had married Robert—I just got fed up. Being in that spot must have had something to do with it. I became edgy, irritable. One after the other, the saleswoman must have brought dozens of coats from all over the store, but none suited me. Either they were too big, or too small, or not of the right fabric, color, or cut.

When we left that store and began to trek toward the center of the shopping district, Shanni said to me, "Why can't you enjoy shopping and getting some nice things for yourself while we're in Helsinki? You know I'm buying." It would have been halfway bearable, if he had just stopped there. But he had to go on. "If you can't enjoy yourself, that's a real flaw."

I exploded. "How can I enjoy myself shopping when I know that I'm returning to the States to no job and to no prospects of getting a job? It doesn't matter who's paying. I just don't like spending money that's not mine. And what I really resent is your self-righteous judgment of my character. Since when did your particular preferences become the Ten Commandments?"

I never bought the coat and there was a lot of tension between us when we went to a cafe to eat lunch. "Unless we talk, this thing is going to get between us. It will not go away by pretending that nothing is wrong," I said, as we sat down with our trays at the cafeteria.

"All I ever wanted to do," Shanni protested, "was to buy a coat for you. I don't see why you make a federal case out of my slightest gesture."

"I have difficulty," I told him, "accepting expensive things from you, especially when I know you don't have much money. You need to understand that I'm not somebody who can enjoy herself at somebody else's expense. But most of all, I hate having my character rearranged by somebody who thinks he knows better than I do what is best for me, and I won't put up with it."

Shanni listened and didn't say anything at the end of my speech. Finally, when we were getting up to leave, he said, "I'm sorry about how this turned out. It's better we end our misery right here." He got up and walked away. Stunned, I watched his back as it disappeared in the crowd. *Oh, God. I've done it again.*

EPILOGUE

1997

"What are these pages and pages in your handwriting?" asked my wife, Rabia.

"Oh, God, where did that come from?" I said. "It's the manuscript of a biography of a woman I once knew, years and years ago. I had forgotten all about it."

"How could you forget about a whole book you wrote? That's incredible to me."

"I know it's hard to believe, but it was an act of mercy on the part of my brain."

"Sounds like the relationship ended painfully."

"It did. But Mayu was a fascinating woman. I was deeply in love with her and she had quite a hold on me."

"She must have been remarkable, if you decided to write about her life."

"She was. But she had a fatal flaw. She systematically sabotaged all of her relationships, and she destroyed ours in the end."

"Tell me more."

"It's all in the manuscript. You can just read it."

"No, no, tell me."

"Well, the last time I saw her was in Finland. We had gone downtown to buy her a coat. I thought I was doing something special for her, but she acted as if I were trying to run her life. It was horrendous. The seeds of destruction had been there all along, but that was when I realized that it wasn't working and was never going to work. I left her and took the next flight out of Finland. When I got back to Washington, I locked away the manuscript on which I had worked so hard for two years and blocked out the memory of her from my mind."

"That's amazing," Rabia said.

"I know. Poor Mayu was a victim of her past. She had received such abominable treatment at the hands of her father and brother that every man was automatically suspect in her eyes. She didn't believe that there was such a thing as pure, honest, and sincere love from a man. I tried to forgive her for how she made me feel—always off-balance and humiliated—and I kept thinking that I could restore her faith in mankind, if I could just love her enough. But things never improved. Instead of making her feel better, I kept feeling worse and worse, myself. That time in Helsinki when we were looking for her coat, things inevitably came to a head."

"And did you ever see her again?"

"No. I didn't want to. Once the hold she had on me was broken, I couldn't believe that I had hung in there for so long. Five years!"

"Do you know what's happened to her since then?"

"Some time ago, I heard that she had remarried and divorced, and gone back to Finland. She was working there as a marriage counselor."

THE END

About the Author

Shahzad Rizvi was born in India, but lives and works in the Washington area. He is the author of *The Last Resident: The Love Story of a British Official and an Indian Princess* and *Dinner with the Dead*, among other novels, stories, and poems. Please visit his websites, www.kahany.org and shahzadrizvi.com for more information.